Sharon could no longer escape her past.

She was sure he wouldn't remember her. She had changed since she was nineteen. Her hair was short now, a softer shade of brown. She was twenty pounds heavier and had replaced her southern accent with a California brogue. Why would he remember her from one night in all of his fifty-one years? He wouldn't want to remember.

He was looking at her like he had twenty-three years ago, with that same expression of inquisitive kindness. She mustn't call him Marcus. She mustn't extend her hand for him to touch. She mustn't say, "Let's talk about our son, Robert, and grieve together."

His face began to swim before her eyes, and she took a deep breath, reminding herself that life was now about Bobby—only Bobby.

YVONNE LEHMAN, an award-winning novelist, lives in the heart of North Carolina's Smoky Mountains with her husband. They are the parents of four grown children. In addition to being an inspirational romance writer, she is also the founder of the Blue Ridge Christian Writers' Conference.

HEARTSONG PRESENTS

After the Storm

Yvonne Lehman

Heartsong Presents

To Lisa, Lori, Cindy, and Howard

Acknowledgment
"To Remember Me" reprinted courtesy of The Living Bank,
P.O. Box 6725, Houston, Texas 77265
Written by Robert N. Test, printed in the Cincinnati Post,
reprinted in Reader's Digest, appeared in "Dear Abby's" syn-
dicated column December 1977

A note from the author:
I love to hear from my readers! You may correspond with me
by writing: **Yvonne Lehman**
Author Relations
PO Box 719
Uhrichsville, OH 44683

ISBN 1-57748-403-7

AFTER THE STORM

Cover illustration by Lauraine Bush.

PRINTED IN THE U.S.A.

one

When the phone rang that evening in her mother's living room, Sharon pushed the remote control button to turn down the TV. She picked up the receiver on the second ring. "Earline Johnson's residence."

"Ma'am, this is the South Carolina State Police. We're trying to locate a Sharon Martin."

Something in his voice made her fingers tighten on the phone. "I'm Sharon Martin." Why would the state police be calling? "Is something wrong?"

"We're on our way to Mount Pleasant, Ms. Martin. Could you tell us which house?"

From U. S. Highway 17, coming from Charleston, there was only one main road into Mount Pleasant, and that was Coleman Boulevard. She gave directions from there. "The third driveway on the right," she said, "but what—"

"We need to talk to you, Ms. Martin. Is anyone with you?"

"Yes," she said instinctively, thinking that this was someone pretending to be the police so that they could find out if she were alone. But her mother lived here alone. Who in the area would know Sharon Martin? "I mean, no."

"We'll be right there, ma'am."

After hearing the click, then a dial tone, Sharon mechanically hung up the phone. She picked up the remote and turned up the volume on *Wheel of Fortune* to

5

try and convince herself everything was all right. Why hadn't the caller said what was wrong?

How did he know to ask for her? *The next of kin* leapt into her mind. Did her mother have a heart attack or something? Or was there an accident? If so, what about Robert? And Karen? And little Bobby? Oh, please, not little Bobby. They had taken him to the petting zoo that afternoon and were going to stop at McDonald's for supper. Did. . . someone choke. . .or something?

Sharon went to the bathroom to brush her hair, as if that mattered should she have to go somewhere. Her soft cotton shirt and matching beige wraparound skirt were presentable. She put on lipstick. Her light blue eyes stared into the mirror at the woman whose face was starkly ashen. Mechanically, she brushed her short brown hair into its usual style—away from her face on one side, and falling softly alongside her face on the other.

You're forty-three years old, Sharon Martin, her mind lectured. *You've lost a husband and survived that. But don't think negative thoughts. Just pray that all is well.*

Her shaky hand put down the brush. The officer hadn't mentioned her mother. He hadn't mentioned anyone. What did that mean? Why couldn't her mother—or Robert—or Karen—call? Why the police? She got her purse from the bedroom.

Her sandaled feet automatically returned her to the living room. The players on TV were smiling. The audience was applauding. Sharon walked to the front screen and held onto the door casing. A line of distant clouds over the horizon formed sleepy eyelids, fast closing over the evening sun. Her knees grew weak so she stepped outside to sit on the porch swing.

The heady scent of magnolias, azaleas, and camellias filled her senses. The chill began to settle on her skin and shiver along her spine. She attributed it to the cooler air that followed the storm which had appeared so suddenly that afternoon. And her mother's home was nearer the ocean than Sharon's home in Los Angeles.

She kept swinging. She kept hugging her arms, even as the sky grayed and twilight fell. Lights appeared in windows of the white clapboard houses set in irregular patterns in this older section of a quiet residential area. A few houses were new, but most had been here for generations. Sharon's grandparents had owned this house, and now her mother.

As Sharon pushed with her foot, the swing swayed, making its usually calming creak. However, an invading uneasiness threatened to permeate her body and mind.

She became acutely aware of the calls of children playing, dogs barking, insects beginning to sing. They always sang louder after a rain. Now they reminded her of the hum of an airplane when she was thousands of miles in the sky, knowing she might as well relax because everything was out of her control. That never stopped her from praying though.

She hardly noticed when night fell.

Finally, car lights appeared. They flashed against trees far down the road, dipped and were lost as they rose and fell at the bottom of the long driveway. Sharon and her friends used to play as though the car lights were eyes of monsters. They'd shoot with clothespin guns and the monster would disappear. Then another would come and meet the same fate.

This one kept coming. It made its way up the drive,

then stopped on the gravel beside the house. Their shoes crunched on the gravel path leading to the front steps. She could see the two uniformed officers clearly until they stepped from the night that had at some point brightened, onto the porch, shadowed by the overhanging roof.

"Looks like nobody's here," said one of them in a deep voice. It must have been the heavyset one. The thinner, taller man touched his arm and turned his head toward Sharon.

"Sorry, ma'am. I didn't see you there," said the first one. The police officer walked closer, took off his cap, and held it with both hands in front of him. His head sort of bowed. "Sharon Martin?" he asked.

"Yes." She would volunteer what information she could. "My mother lives here. She's Earline Johnson."

He looked sad. His voice was even and sympathetic. "There's been an accident."

Sharon nodded, dreamlike, in that state somewhere between disbelief and reality. She'd been there before—several times. She'd known then, too, but it still had to be confirmed. She was older now. Better able to deal with life's blows—perhaps. She drew in a breath. "How bad?"

"Your mother was killed. Also, Robert and Karen Martin."

Just. . .words, she told herself. *My mother. Robert. . .son of my flesh. . .my young, beautiful, precious son. His wife. No!* She tried to shake her head, but it wouldn't move. Her unblinking eyes stared at her fingers, clenched into fists.

Suddenly, heavy thick air seared her paralyzed throat and settled like hot lead across her chest. Her head came up. *Please God, leave me something.* Her luminous eyes searched the shadowed figures. "Bobby?" she whispered.

"He's in the hospital. We can take you there."

"Yes," Sharon breathed. "Thank you." She stood, lost her balance, but the officer's hand came out to steady her.

"I'm sorry," she said.

"It's all right."

They went inside with her. Sharon picked up the remote, but the buttons looked blurry, so she walked over to the TV where everyone was still smiling and applauding and the wheel was still turning. It had seemed like an eternity for Sharon since that phone call. She pushed the off button.

The officer picked up her purse from the couch. "Is this yours?"

She took it.

"Can we lock up for you, or anything?"

A sound came from Sharon's throat. *Lock up? Why? What was there that mattered? Things!* "The door locks when it closes."

She hurried outside, trying not to look. Her disobedient glance saw the door close. She heard the lock click.

She swayed. The anticipating officer grasped her elbow. *Focus on the window,* she told herself. Somewhere she'd heard that when a door closes, a window opens.

She feared the answer but had to ask, "Is Bobby badly hurt?"

two

After reviewing all the information, Helen Gamble, a tall thin woman wearing white, unlocked the door to the small room in one corner of the emergency room. Perspiration formed on her brow, despite the cold chills running up her spine.

Officer Leland had called from Mount Pleasant, saying he was bringing in Sharon Martin. During the fifteen years she'd been nursing supervisor, Helen had never faced the almost impossible task of confronting someone who had just lost not one, not two, but three—three loved ones. No amount of training or experience could prepare her for this.

Helen had lost her father when she was twenty-three and later felt she could empathize with the grieving and bereaved. But no way could she empathize with Sharon Martin. And how was she going to give the woman hope, yet be honest about that small boy whose chances were so slim? She prayed the little boy would not die before she went off duty at eleven. She'd quit her job before telling that woman she had nobody left alive.

Helen flipped the switch that flooded the small room with recessed fluorescent light. Her eyes swept over the muted brown-toned carpet, the lighter couch that looked like stiff, brushed tweed, its matching armchairs, the arrangement of faded paper flowers on the low wooden table, the two watercolor prints of pastel blooms without stems on the wall above the couch. The intent was to provide comfort, peace, stability, and easy cleaning.

The bereaved woman wouldn't really see it, Helen told herself—nor would she care. That was soon confirmed by the dazed look on Sharon Martin's face when she hurried through the door, flanked by two officers Helen recognized as Leland and Burris. Helen's professionalism clicked in, and she walked toward Sharon, a woman about her own age.

"This is Sharon Martin," Leland said.

Helen nodded. "I am Helen Gamble, the nursing supervisor."

"Can I see Bobby?" asked the distraught woman.

"Not just yet, Mrs. Martin. Let's go in here and sit down." Helen gestured toward the small room. "We can talk in there."

Swiftly Sharon headed for the room.

"Is there anything else we can do?" asked Leland.

"No, thank you," Helen replied, seeing both regret and relief in the officers' eyes before they walked away. She knew they were sorry about this terrible tragedy yet relieved to be free of its burden. They could go now, relive it and talk about it for awhile, tell their families, and eventually put it away in the back of their minds where it belonged. Helen would have to live with it a while longer. Sharon would have to live with it forever.

❧

Sharon sat on the edge of the couch as the nursing supervisor—had she said her name was Helen?—said a few words with the officers. She braced herself as she watched Helen cross the room and sit beside her on the couch. Her mind barely registered the gentle pressure of the woman's hands when she reached to clasp Sharon's. Sharon blinked, trying to keep her hot tears from spilling down her face. She had to hold herself together for Bobby's sake.

"What did the police officers tell you?" Helen asked.

"Not very much," Sharon answered, lowering her head. *Not much? Only that Robert, and Karen, and Mother. . . What did the officer say? Something about the storm. Blinding rain. High winds. Maybe the car, or the tractor-trailer, hydroplaned on the rain-soaked highway. They didn't know details.*

Sharon looked up into the caring gray eyes, the kindly mature face of Helen Gamble. "They said. . .that Bobby is alive."

"Bobby is in surgery now," Helen said softly. "I can't tell you much more than that. He's in the best of hands," she said, trying to console. "Dr. Paul Thomas is one of our finest pediatric surgeons. Three other members of his team are assisting. Everything possible is being done."

Sharon nodded. "He has to be all right," she choked.

Helen nodded too, and brushed at the wetness rolling down her cheeks. "I'm sorry," she said, letting go of Sharon's hands. She stood and reached into her pocket for a package of tissue.

"Don't apologize," Sharon replied with a trembly smile, taking the tissue Helen held out to her. "Thank you. . .for being here."

Helen gently placed her hand on Sharon's shoulder. "Sharon, do you happen to have type AB-negative blood?"

"I don't," Sharon replied fearfully. "That's Bobby's type! Surely you have it or can get it."

"Oh, yes. That's no problem," Helen quickly assured

her, returning to the couch. "I just thought you might prefer to donate if you had his type."

"You'll let me know if you don't get a donor?" Sharon pled. She grabbed Helen's hand. "Promise me Bobby will have the needed blood. You won't let the supply get too low. Promise me."

"Yes, Sharon, yes, I promise," Helen said before Sharon could even finish her plea. She paused, and Sharon braced herself for more bad news.

"Sharon, there's another matter that I have to bring up."

"Another matter?"

Helen took a deep breath. "It's about organ donation, Sharon."

Sharon stared blankly in front of her. Organ donation? Did Bobby need an organ? "If I have anything he needs. . ."

"No, I mean. . ." Helen swallowed hard. "Your other family members. Robert's driver's license indicates he is a donor. However, we consult family members about this."

Sharon continued to stare. A look of horror crossed her face. She understood. She rose from the couch and gazed at the flowers without stems. After a long moment her head slowly turned and looked down at Helen. She tried to think of anything—but that. Then the head moved, and Helen's eyes met hers.

"We have to know soon," said the pale woman in white.

So others can live, Sharon was thinking. No, she wasn't really thinking. Inadvertently thoughts of Robert, Karen, and her mother tripped across her mind. She sat down again.

"My mother mentioned it one time. When her driver's license was renewed they asked her if she wanted to be a donor. She laughed and said she was too old."

"She isn't," Helen said quietly. "What can't be used on patients can be used in research in medical schools."

Sharon's mind leaped back to high school days. Some students had laughed and others had vomited when they dissected frogs. She felt, now, like she might do one or the other. "Robert and Karen are so young. But it's the kind of thing they would want to do when they were older. . . They were such good kids."

"I'm sure they were," Helen responded.

"I don't know," Sharon said distantly. "I don't know if they should be donors. I know it would help others, but. . . they're. . .my family."

Helen nodded, and Sharon noticed that the woman didn't push her one way or the other. "Is there anyone I can call for you?" Helen asked. "Relatives?"

"My mother has a sister in Wisconsin who's in a nursing home. She has Alzheimer's. I'm the only other relative that Robert has."

"And Robert's wife?" Helen asked.

Sharon's mouth fell open. She felt a wave of shock. "Karen's parents," she said in a whisper. "I have not thought. . . they have to be told."

"Where do they live, Sharon?"

"California. Los Angeles."

"There's a time difference. Would anyone be home?"

Sharon looked at her watch. James Davis owned a small accounting firm. He usually got home around six o'clock. Occasionally, his wife, Mary, helped out in the office. School was out and their teenagers could be anywhere. "Mary might be home," she said. "But I wouldn't want to tell her this if she's alone."

"It might be wise to wait," Helen agreed.

Sharon had mixed emotions. She didn't want to be the bearer of such tragic news. But it had to be done. And she was the only one who could do it. There were arrangements to make. She turned a pallid face to Helen. "Where. . .are they?" she asked.

Helen took a deep breath before answering. "They're in the ER on life support to keep the organs alive," she said with difficulty. "Would you like to see them?"

"No!" Sharon said immediately, then just as quickly said, "Yes!" She shook her head. "I don't know."

"That's all right. You don't have to decide now. Think about it." Helen paused, adding softly, "When you can. There's a waiting room outside Pediatric ICU. That's where Bobby will be taken after surgery. Or you could go to the chapel."

Sharon didn't want any of that. She wanted her family. She wanted to see Bobby. She didn't want to be making these decisions. Her options were limited. "Where is the chapel?"

Helen led her down the hall to a door with a cross on it. "I'll stay with you, if you like."

"I'd like to be alone for awhile," Sharon told her.

Helen handed her the package of tissues. "I'll be back later," she promised. "We also have a chaplain who will come by as soon as he can."

"Thank you," Sharon said. She stepped inside and closed the door.

She wanted to escape—escape from Helen's words. *"They're in the ER,"* she'd said. *All this talk about organs. . . being cut apart. . .my dear Robert. . .sweet Karen. . .my own mother. . .and yet. . .and yet. . .someone needs to donate blood for Bobby. What would happen if they didn't?*

And. . .and. . .do I never see them again? Do I remember them as they were? Or. . .see them. . .mangled? I don't know! I don't know!

Her eyes squeezed shut. Her fingers came up and grabbed bunches of hair from each side of her head. Her hands pulled—pulled as if trying to force out some answers from her mind. No answers came. Only pain. Slowly her grip loosened. Her hands fell limply to her sides. Her eyes opened.

For an instant, while her eyes adjusted to the different surroundings, she saw only the far wall where light radiated from behind a huge cross that reached to where crossbeams met at the apex of the ceiling. Facing that symbol of omniscient power, she felt afraid and uncertain. When Mitchell died, she'd found comfort, peace, acceptance. But this. . . this was too much. Darkness and despair threatened to overwhelm her.

As the room came into focus, she walked unsteadily down the narrow carpeted aisle that separated several rows of rich mahogany pews. About halfway down, she slid into one.

With her eyes fixed on the cross, she remembered when she'd been a young, single, frightened girl and had prayed that she wouldn't be pregnant. But she had been. Robert had been born. She'd been blessed with him for twenty-two years. She wanted him longer. But he was gone.

"Gone," she whispered in the awesome silence. "How can I stand it?"

Then, like a voice speaking in the dreadful silence, she saw the words inscribed in gold. The wooden strip along the wall below the cross read, "Come unto me, all ye that labour and are heavy laden, and I will give you rest. Matthew 11:28."

The realization was as clear as if the words had been spoken: If there was no help here. . .then there was none. . . anywhere.

Trembling, Sharon grasped the back of the pew in front of her and stood. With unsteady steps she moved to the kneeling pad below the raised dais. She fell to her knees and looked up at the cross for a timeless moment.

With a cry, her hands clenched, her forearms reached out onto the dais, and her forehead touched the carpet between them.

"Please, help Bobby. Help. . .me," she implored weakly. And she sobbed—like a helpless child who needed to be cradled in her Father's arms.

three

After her desolate wails subsided, Sharon lay drained.
With her face turned away from the door and feeling an
incredible sense of helplessness, she allowed blessed
blackness to overtake her.

A long time later, she heard a voice calling her out of
the enveloping darkness, but her mind and body rebelled
against it. Finally, sensing the urgency in the voice,
Sharon tried to open her eyes, tried to move her limbs, but
felt void of the ability to react.

Slowly, sensations began to come. Her eyes could move
beneath closed lids. They did not want to open—did not
want to see. Her hair felt wet and matted against the side
of her face that lay against the carpet. She heard a raspy
sound, then realized her mouth was open, taking in air
down a dry and parched throat.

Why couldn't she move? Or feel anything? How long
had she lain in that contorted position—half sitting, half
lying? She willed her arms to move, but they lay lifeless
against the nubby surface of the carpet. Her fingers tightly
clutched a wet tissue.

She felt hands on her back, gently shaking, while a
masculine voice demanded, "Mrs. Martin. Wake up. Wake
up, Mrs. Martin."

Her eyes slowly opened. She saw the paneled wall. The
cross. She felt cold. The hands felt warm. Then as the
blood began to course through her veins like pinpricks,

the flood of memory ripped through her heart.

Flinching, she closed her eyes again. But the insistent voice kept saying her name and the hands tried to move her arms. Had she fallen asleep? Or lost consciousness? What time was it? There was something she had to do. . .

And who was this person, forcing her awake? She moaned softly, and the hands moved away. She missed their warmth, their strength. She managed to lift her head and turn her face toward the intruder.

Kneeling beside her was a dark-haired man with a pleasant face and kind, sympathetic eyes. He wore a light green smock and had a face mask around his neck. "I'm Dr. Paul Thomas," he said gently.

The doctor? "Bobby?" she whimpered. If Bobby wasn't all right, she would have no reason to move from this spot. No reason to go on.

"He came through the surgery well," the doctor said, his eyes avoiding hers.

Sharon saw the gentle pain in the man's averted face. Something was wrong. But he said Bobby came through. . . "He's going to be all right?"

"Here, let me help you," he said, as Sharon managed to rise to a sitting position. She welcomed his assistance as she stood up on shaky legs. He helped her to the first pew. Sharon brushed back the strands of damp hair that had stuck to her face. She must look a fright. But that didn't matter.

"May I see him?" she asked.

"After he's taken to ICU," Dr. Thomas said. "Someone will let you know."

"He'll need me," she said.

Dr. Thomas nodded, but his moment of hesitation told

Sharon there was more. Then he explained. "He hasn't regained consciousness."

"You mean, he's in a coma?"

He nodded. "We're doing everything we can for him, Mrs. Martin. But it's basically out of our hands now."

She looked at him with frightened eyes. "But he will. . . recover. Won't he?"

She noticed the doctor pause, as if he were choosing his words with great care. "His being young and healthy is in his favor, Mrs. Martin. But being young and having so much trauma is against him too. We can only wait. And pray."

"How badly is he hurt?"

Before he could answer, the overhead page sounded. "Dr. Thomas, 5534, Stat!"

"Excuse me," he said, "I'll get back with you." He jumped up and ran up the aisle as the page was repeated.

Sharon followed. When she reached the door, she heard the page again. "Bobby," she said weakly, standing in the doorway with the door pressed against her. The doctor disappeared around a corner, just as a man and woman appeared.

The man introduced himself as John Cameron, hospital chaplain, and the woman as Beth Frame, hospital social worker.

"It's Bobby, isn't it?" Sharon asked, desperation in her voice.

"I can't say, Mrs. Martin," the chaplain replied gently. "But it's my understanding the pediatric surgeon is in with Bobby and will speak with you soon."

Beth put her arms around Sharon's shoulders. "Come on, you need a cup of coffee."

Sharon welcomed any diversion. They led her to a room behind a nurses' station, and she accepted the coffee. Why she said it, she wasn't sure—maybe because she had to keep her mind and body busy with something—but as soon as she sat on the couch, she lifted her eyes to Beth.

"Could you tell me more about organ donation?" Maybe it was a deep inner feeling that her loved ones had to live. . . somehow.

Beth handed Sharon some material.

She read.

To Remember Me

The day will come when. . .at a certain moment a doctor will determine that. . .for all intents and purposes, my life has stopped. When that happens, do not attempt to instill artificial life into my body by the use of a machine. And don't call this my deathbed. Let it be called the Bed of Life, and let my body be taken from it to help others lead fuller lives.

Give my sight to the man who has never seen a sunrise, a baby's face, or love in the eyes of a woman.

Give my heart to a person whose own heart has caused nothing but endless days of pain.

Give my blood to the teenager who was pulled from the wreckage of his car, so that he might live to see his grandchildren play.

Give my kidneys to one who depends on a machine to exist from week to week.

Take my bones, every muscle, every fiber and nerve in my body and find a way to make a crippled child walk.

*Explore every corner of my brain. Take my
cells, if necessary, and let them grow so that,
someday, a speechless boy will shout at the crack
of a bat and a deaf girl will hear the sound of rain
against her window.*

*Burn what is left of me and scatter the ashes to
the winds to help the flowers grow.*

*If you must bury something, let it be my faults,
my weaknesses, and all prejudice against my
fellow man. . . .*

Give my soul to God.

*If by chance, you wish to remember me, do it
with a kind deed or word to someone who needs
you. . . .*

Sharon lifted her tear-filled eyes. "Do I need to sign
something?"

"Yes, for your mother and Robert," John replied, "but
Karen's parents will need to make the decision about her."

Sharon realized that's why time had meant something to
her earlier. They would probably be home now. "I must
call them."

"Here," Beth said kindly. "Sit at my desk."

Sharon went over and sat in the swivel armchair. She
reached for the phone, tried to press the buttons, but her
hand was shaking so much she couldn't touch the right
buttons. She looked up at John with a stark face, about to
crumble.

"I'll do it," Beth offered.

Sharon automatically recalled the numbers like one who
had been accustomed to calling them often. When the
phone rang, Beth handed the receiver to Sharon.

"Hello," sounded the bright, cheerful voice of fifteen-year-old Kim.

"Kim, honey, let me speak to your mother."

"Is this Sharon?"

"Yes, honey. Get your mother, please."

"Mom!" she yelled. "It's Sharon. Hurry, it's long distance. She'll be right here. How's it going?"

Sharon inhaled sharply. "Not well, honey."

"What's wrong?" Her voice faded. "Mom, something's wrong."

"Sharon?"

"Mary," Sharon began, and her voice caught in her throat.

"Sharon, what is it? Is something wrong?"

"Yes, Mary. Maybe you'd better get James."

"He's right here. We were eating dinner."

Sharon could hear James's voice in the background asking, "What is it?"

Sharon didn't know any other way. She had to say it. "I'm at the hospital, Mary. Bobby's hurt bad."

"Oh, no," Mary moaned. "What happened?"

"There was an accident. Robert and Karen and. . . Mother. They were all in the car, Mary."

"Are they hurt?" she asked.

"Yes. No. Oh, Mary. they're. . .gone."

"Gone? No! Sharon, no! James!" Mary screamed as she dropped the phone. She wouldn't stop screaming. Sharon moved the phone away from her ear and put her head on the desk and sobbed aloud.

Beth took the phone. James Davis got on, and Beth told him what details she could. He asked to speak with Sharon. It was distressful, but comforting, talking with James.

His voice was strained, but he talked of things that had to be done, giving Sharon a sense of direction. "Yes, I'll call as soon as I know anything more about Bobby," she promised.

She told him she had decided to donate Robert's and her mother's organs. James said to fax the donor information to his office. Sharon sighed with relief at that. Yes, that was a way for instant communication. She was not quite so alone anymore.

"I have to go to Mary now, Sharon. Just be strong for Bobby, and we'll be in touch."

As she hung up the receiver, a longing for Mitchell surged through Sharon with an intensity she'd never felt before. He'd been a stabilizing factor in her life since she'd married him when Robert was five years old. He'd been her strength while she grieved for her father. He'd given his blessing to Robert's marrying so young, while she had been reluctant. Now she was glad, so glad, that Robert had those few years of happiness with Karen and Bobby.

Oh, Robert, Robert, my son. Mitchell, why can't I be strong like you? Oh, God, how can I do this alone?

Suddenly a knock sounded and the door opened. Dr. Thomas stepped into the room, and Sharon's first thought was that he'd come to report on Bobby. It hadn't been long since he'd been called away for the emergency that must surely have involved her grandson.

Then a younger man stepped in behind Dr. Thomas. He, too, wore a green smock, and a face mask hung around his neck. Her eyes riveted to the younger man's face. Dr. Thomas was making introductions, saying something about blood, even mentioning Bobby. But Sharon couldn't make out the words, couldn't hear above the hammering of her heart and the churning of her emotions.

She could not take her eyes from the young man. He wouldn't know her—but she knew him. And just what was this? Some cruel twist of fate to sever the last thin threads of her emotional stability?

For an instant, even thoughts of Bobby receded to the back of her mind. All she could think of was this young man to whom she needed no introduction, a man she had never expected to face, a man who by walking into this room became a part of her living nightmare—a man she knew was Dr. Luke Sinclair.

Sharon hadn't thought her distress could be any greater. But now, in addition to her concern about Bobby, a reminder of her past sins had walked into the room in the form of Dr. Luke Sinclair, the son of Marcus Sinclair.

Oh God, is this punishment or blessing?

Forcing her thoughts away from the past, Sharon reminded herself that God had forgiven her. Past sins—or even someone learning about them—were not the most important factor here. Bobby was!

She felt Beth's hands on her shoulders, gently leading her to sit on the couch beside Chaplain John. The kind woman handed her a small cup of water. Sharon took a sip, then forced herself to listen as Dr. Thomas took a chair near the couch and Luke Sinclair sat on the edge of the couch, near her.

Dr. Thomas described Bobby's injuries, most of which were common in extensive trauma such as automobile accidents. "The spleen developed a hematoma that ruptured. Bleeding became profuse. We removed his spleen and stopped the bleeding."

"He has a rare blood type," Sharon said, concerned.

"Members of my own family have the same type," Luke said. "Rest assured, there is plenty available."

"The surgery was successful, Mrs. Martin," Dr. Thomas added. "And Bobby is getting the best of care."

"When can I see him?" Sharon asked.

Dr. Thomas explained that Bobby was in recovery. "After he's taken to ICU, you may see him for a few minutes. But you can't stay. His heart rate, blood pressure, and cerebral pressure will be monitored constantly. He will have IVs and a catheter for draining urine. But children are resilient, Mrs. Martin. We expect that within three to five days he will move to a semiprivate room and you may stay with him then if you wish."

Sharon nodded. "I need to let him know I'm with him."

She could tell by the distressed expression Dr. Thomas couldn't hide that something was wrong. She looked at Luke.

"Mrs. Martin," he began, and she dreaded what was to follow, hearing sympathy in his voice. "We suspect head trauma. We can't be sure when he will regain consciousness. It's too soon to know the extent of the damage. That's why the swelling and pressure in the brain is being monitored, so we will know immediately if it gets too high."

"And if it does?" Sharon asked, frightened.

"Then we would go to surgery and put in a shunt to relieve the fluid and blood pressure."

Sharon went numb. Her mind and emotions were battling each other. A part of her wanted to see Bobby, hug him, tell him she loved him, see for herself that he was all right. Another part was glad he was oblivious to all this and that she didn't have to tell him that his world was shattered. How could she ever do that?

"Is there anything we can do for you, Mrs. Martin?" Dr. Thomas was asking. "I mean personally. Someone we can call?"

Before Sharon could answer, Beth said that Earline Johnson's pastor had called. He and his wife were on their way to the hospital.

"I'm also available," Chaplain John said, with a kind smile.

Sharon was grateful. But what could they do? What could anyone do? Then she remembered. "He has a favorite toy—a stuffed Barney dinosaur. He took it with him everywhere. Do you know if. . .if that is. . .somewhere? When he wakes up, he will need that. . .to hug."

"I'll find out," Dr. Luke Sinclair replied immediately. "I'll personally see that he gets a dinosaur."

Sharon's eyes closed on the pain. Bobby would never see his mom or dad again. He would never see his great-grandmother again.

When Bobby woke up, all he would see was a stuffed dinosaur.

⋧

Less than an hour later, with the Rev. John and Nancy Clark at her side, Beth told Sharon that Bobby was settled in ICU and she could see him for a few minutes. Beth led her to the unit, where Luke Sinclair and a young woman he introduced as his assistant, Julie, awaited her.

"Has there been any change?"

"No, but that's a good sign," Luke assured her. "His system needs time to recover from the shock it's had."

Sharon nodded. Her eyes swept around the circle of rooms, most of which had curtains pushed aside so the children could be observed at all times from the circular nurses' station. Julie took Sharon by the arm and led her into a small room. "May I talk to him?" Sharon asked.

"For a moment," Julie replied, and drew up a chair for Sharon, who sat and rubbed her hands together until her fingers felt warm, then reached through the high railing to touch a spot on Bobby's arm that was not bruised or near where the IV's were stuck in. She didn't know if he could hear her but felt he would sense her presence.

His hair appeared darker than usual, surrounding his face that appeared so ghostly white on the bed, without a pillow. His little lips that hadn't been still since he learned to communicate in his own special language, now lay motionless, parted slightly, but she could not tell if he breathed. She could not see the white blanket move. The place on his arm felt cold to her touch.

Sharon cleared her throat and tried to speak calmly, softly. "Grandmother is here with you, Bobby. I love you more than anything in the whole world. I know you're not feeling well right now, but there are a lot of people who will help you get better. Everything's going to be all right."

In a soft, low voice, while letting him feel the warmth of her touch, Sharon reminded Bobby of the special love that had existed between them from the time he was born. His parents had lived with Sharon while Karen worked and Robert was completing his education. It had been Sharon who heard Bobby's first word, encouraged him in taking his first step, taught him his first swimming strokes in the pool. She'd kissed his hurts and bandaged them with cartoon character Band-Aids.

She'd discovered anew the wonder and mystery of the

world—the purpose of rain, the joy of sunshine, the beauty of a yellow moon, the excitement of finding tiny ants and miniature flowers usually so far away from an adult's eyes. She'd taught him the most simple, most profound answers to life's mysteries: God made them. He loves us.

"And I know, Bobby, why I'm called a grandmother. The grandest time of my life has been spent mothering you. My darling, I love you, and I'll take care of you."

She didn't know how long she'd been talking, perhaps to herself as much as to Bobby, when she felt strong, gentle fingers curl over one shoulder. She looked up to see the kind face, the caring eyes, that resembled her Robert, and she moved her hand away from Bobby, fearing he might feel the tremor of emotion that spread through her.

"We have to ask you to leave now, Mrs. Martin," Luke Sinclair said gently. "You may see him again in the morning. But tonight, he will be monitored and watched constantly."

"Yes," Julie said, coming further into the room. "I will be with him for several hours, and I'm on call. You might try and get some rest."

Reluctantly, Sharon left the room. Beth was still waiting for her.

"Beth, I can't leave the hospital tonight."

"I know," Beth replied, taking Sharon's arm and steering her toward the elevator.

four

Seeing lights flash against the drapes as a car came up the drive late that evening, Trish Sinclair walked into the foyer. Luke was unlocking the front door to let himself in.

Except for Beethoven's Fifth playing softly in the background, all was quiet. "I'm beat," Luke groaned, setting his bag down and loosening his tie.

"Story of your life, huh?" Trish said with a smile, coming over to him in her cream silk robe that he used to love to touch, saying her skin was even more delectable to his caress. Her face tilted toward his, and her blond hair fell below her shoulders as she began to help unbutton his shirt.

He didn't quite meet her eyes. "Let me get a shower, then we'll talk," he said, and hurried from the room.

"Story of my life," Trish muttered under her breath, her eyes clouding like a blue sky turning gray. He didn't even notice that her hair was not in its usual ponytail. Or that she wasn't wearing jeans, a T-shirt, and tennis shoes.

She was in the kitchen, taking dishes out of the dishwasher when he returned from his shower, fully clad in pajamas and towel-drying his dark waves into mussed curls that accentuated his rugged handsomeness.

Trish determined not to argue. The children were asleep. It was just the two of them—alone. "Had dinner?"

"No, but all I want right now is to unwind a little."

Trish followed him into his study and sat on the couch,

drawing her legs underneath her, while he tossed the towel onto his leather desk chair, sank into his recliner, and leaned his head back, closing his eyes.

"It was rough, Trish," he said, sighing heavily. "We had to operate on a little two-year-old boy."

"Was Julie there?"

He detected the edge to her voice.

A muscle tightened in his jaw.

"She's my assistant, Trish," he said blandly, opening his eyes.

Trish shrugged. "Even doctors get a day off now and then! Don't they? Seems I remember when you and I had a life."

He glanced toward the ceiling, his brow wrinkling. "That's not fair, Trish. You didn't come into this marriage with your eyes closed. Your own dad was a doctor."

"I know, Luke," she said defensively. "I know your work is important and necessary. But I need something for myself."

His heavy brows formed a straight line as he scowled. "I don't understand you, Trish. I've given you this nice home—two wonderful boys—I don't make any unreasonable demands of you." He spread his hands. "I don't want this kind of thing when I come home worn-out from the hospital."

"Well, what about me?" Her voice rose and she jumped from the couch. "You think I'm not worn-out? Day after day running after two nonstop boys? At least you get to sit down once in awhile!"

At his exasperated expression she stalked over to the chair and grabbed the damp towel. "I pick up after the boys all day long. Then you come home and I have to pick up after you too." She threw it on the floor. "Well, I won't! And I won't be ignored. You never ask about my day, or the boys'. All you want to talk about is yourself and the hospital."

"Trish, I need to be able to relax and unwind before I can go to sleep."

Her lip trembled. "You used to call me your sleeping pill."

He could not meet her eyes. Finally he mumbled, "You've changed, Trish. I guess maybe you're tired. I've told you over and over you can hire somebody to help out around here."

"I don't need somebody to help," she shot back. "I need. . .to be appreciated. I mean, I spent all week cleaning this house and planning for this evening, cooking a special dinner for you and Marcus."

His head came up. "Was Dad upset?"

Trish snorted. "Your dad is never upset, Luke. He's a rock. He and the boys frolicked all over the backyard this afternoon while I cooked. It was really relaxing for me."

"Then why are you so tired? Do you need vitamins or something?"

"A doctor should recognize the signs, Luke. Maybe I'm depressed. Maybe I think a father should be home once in awhile to do those things with his children, instead of a grandfather. Maybe I think I should be eating dinner with my husband, not with his dad."

"I'm sorry," Luke said and reached over to his desk for the remote control. "Let's catch the news. Maybe then, you'll understand why I had to stay, and why I'm tired."

Trish returned to the couch and sat stiffly. As the news-caster reported the horrible tragedy, the dead people, the little boy hanging by a slim thread of hope, she felt a stab of guilt.

"You operated on that little boy?" Trish whispered when the report ended.

"I assisted Paul," he said. "Then I talked with Sharon Martin. All of it, Trish—it just took everything out of me."

"I'm sorry," she said repentantly, tears in her eyes for what her husband had gone through. Tears because she hadn't been helpful. Tears for the family's tragedy, for the little boy, and for her own husband, who after a trying day, tried to ease the mind of a suffering woman. Luke was a good man. She should not be so hard on him.

"I'm sorry too, Trish," he said. "I'll try to be a better husband and father."

"You're okay," she said contritely. *But why this tension between us? Why aren't we able to communicate anymore? Why couldn't it be like it used to be?* "I'll check on the boys, then I'd better hit the hay."

"Be there in a little while," he said. "I'll call Dad and apologize for missing dinner."

"You don't think it's too late?"

"He always watches the late news."

Trish nodded and left the room.

Luke sat on the edge of the chair, fingering the remote control. He grimaced. He tried to leave his work at the hospital—wanted to have the kind of camaraderie he and Trish used to have—but things changed. People changed.

Turning off the television, he forced his thoughts to the matter at hand, went to his desk chair, and reached for the telephone.

❧

Fifty-one-year-old Criminal Court Judge Marcus Sinclair

sat in his den at the back of his historic Charleston home, watching the late news and having a snack of skim milk and a piece of Trish's famous low-cal banana nut bread she'd sent home with him. It had been a good evening with her and his grandchildren. Would have been better had Luke joined them.

Then the report of the Martin family caught his complete attention. *Terrible tragedy,* crossed his mind. The same phrase had run through his mind many times, including that very afternoon as he reviewed the files of a murder case.

Just before the sportscast, the phone rang.

Running his hand through his still-dark hair, Marcus smiled when he heard Luke's voice, apologizing for not being able to make it for dinner.

"We had an emergency, Dad." Luke told him about Bobby. "I donated blood. Bobby has the rare type that you and I have."

Marcus frowned. "Is the supply low, Son? I could—"

"No, no. There's ample supply for the time being. Of course, when you have a chance, it would be helpful in case of need later on."

Marcus heard the strain in Luke's voice. "I'll donate soon, Son."

"Dad. There is something you might do. Your being a judge carries a little clout."

"Does it?" Marcus said in a light tone. "With my own children?"

"Well," Luke retracted with a small laugh, "at least in a courtroom."

"Okay, what can I do?"

Luke told him about the Barney dinosaur. "You suppose

you could find out if the police picked it up or if it's in the car. It was Bobby's favorite toy and his grandmother thinks it might help."

Marcus grimaced at the sadness in Luke's voice. He did sound drained. "I can do better than that, Son. I'll go to the station and find that dinosaur, if possible. If it's not in good shape, I'll try and get one like it."

"Thanks, Dad. Again, I'm sorry I missed dinner tonight. I'm sure Trish and the children enjoyed your being there."

"Trish cooked a great meal, Luke. The kids and I had fun. But I think Trish is worried about your working too hard. Says you don't get enough rest."

"Dad, that's the life of a doctor. She knows that."

"Yeah, well. Try and take a little time for yourselves, Luke. That's important."

"Sure, Dad."

After they hung up, Marcus stared blankly at the TV. He'd noticed Trish's pain that afternoon. How could he miss it? It echoed so strongly the look he'd seen in his dear wife's eyes so many years ago. Would his own silence lead Luke to repeat those mistakes of the past?

five

After the Rev. John Clark and his wife, Nancy, left, the nursing supervisor Helen reappeared. She told Sharon that she could stay in the room behind her office and lie on the couch. The night-shift head nurse would let her know the moment there was any change and when she could see Bobby. Helen got a pillow and blanket. "Lie down," she insisted.

Too distraught to do anything but obey, Sharon lay on the couch with her knees drawn up. Helen placed the blanket over her. "Try and rest," she said. "Could I go to your home and get anything for you?"

"No," Sharon said. "The preacher's wife said she would come in the morning and take me home. There will be so much to do."

"Don't think about it right now, Sharon. Just rest and be ready for Bobby."

"Yes," Sharon said. "Thank you."

Helen touched her shoulder, then walked out of the room and to the desk. Sharon could hear her giving instructions to the head nurse.

Sharon prayed. That always helped, to know that God was near, that He cared, that He could take the mess people made out of things and bring some good from it. Oh, how wonderfully well He'd done that twenty-three years ago when the girl inside her died and a woman began to emerge. Her thoughts drifted back in time.

··

Sharon had been nineteen years old. Her parents had presented her with the news that her father was divorcing her mother and transferring to California with his secretary, fifteen years his junior, who would become his new wife.

There'd be no money for her second year of college, and it was too late for her to take advantage of any scholarships or apply for financial aid. Her boyfriend found the situation deplorable. It didn't fit in with the plans he had for his future. A girl with divorced parents seemed flawed to him, as if it were her somehow her fault. Sharon wondered if it were. Had her dreams, her plans, her hopes for college been too much for her parents to deal with?

Her boyfriend looked different then—as did her dad. She lost trust in men and had to face the fact that she didn't really know her parents. What she thought was a stable family was not. What she thought was a secure future with her boyfriend was not. Life was cruel, unfair.

She'd decided to ignore her feelings and instead had accepted an invitation to a friend's beach party. For the first time in her life, she accepted an alcoholic drink. But the party wasn't fun. Instead of feeling elated, Sharon felt only more depressed. Unable to join in the festivities, she wandered down the sandy shore until she came to an outcropping of rock in front of a darkened cottage. She climbed up onto the rocks and looked out over the billowing waves of the ocean, oblivious to the gathering storm clouds in the night sky and the cool breeze that stirred her hair, as if giving flight to the long strands.

The sea became rough, the night dark and stormy. The warm wetness on her face turned cold. She climbed down and walked toward the ocean, oblivious to the falling rain, stopping only when the waves splashed against her knees and she could feel the cold and the pull of the unstable sandy floor as it encouraged her to become part of that vast ocean.

The rain beat harder. A thunderclap was followed by a streak of light far out over the water. She turned away from the beckoning waves, stumbled, and felt strong arms helping her to rise.

"Come on," he said gently, and she leaned against him as he held onto her shoulders and told her to put her arm around his waist since her feet were unsteady. The thunder and lightning came closer, and he made her run to the beach house. He handed her a towel for her wet hair and demanded that she dry off and change into a terry cloth robe while her clothes dried.

When she returned to the front room, a fire was burning in the fireplace. He took an afghan from the back of the couch and put it around her shoulders, then gently motioned toward the couch, opposite the fireplace, where she snuggled into its corner against a cushion. He brought a rack from somewhere and arranged her clothes on it to dry near the fire.

The man sat in a chair where the firelight was not directly on his face. He asked what had brought her out on such a stormy night, and she poured out the story of her family, her boyfriend, and the reasons she left the party. Slowly she became aware of him as a person, as a man, as one who was older than the college boys she knew.

"What's. . .your name?" she asked hesitantly.

He didn't answer immediately, instead rising to poke the fire. He threw on another log, then glanced at her and said his name. He looked at her expectantly, as if waiting for her name in turn.

She didn't want to be herself—Sharon Ann Johnson. She didn't want him to know she was only nineteen, so she said she was in college, her age was twenty-one. "My name," she said, feeling like the different person she wanted to be, "is Angela."

She took the glass of wine he offered and welcomed the escape from her troubles. While the rain beat against the windowpanes and blotted out the world, she focused her attention only on the handsome man who seemed to care about what was happening to her. He seemed to understand. Concern deepened his dark eyes. To avoid her growing awareness of him, she looked around and noticed a cupcake with a candle stuck in the middle of it on the coffee table. "What is that?" she asked.

A scoff accompanied his laugh. "A friend's idea of cheering me up. That's my birthday present."

"This is your birthday?"

He looked at his watch. "For at least another hour."

"How old are you?"

"Twenty-eight."

Now she was glad she'd said she was twenty-one. Why, she wasn't sure. Maybe she felt he wouldn't have given her the numbing glass of wine if he knew she was only nineteen. Maybe he would consider her just a child. She'd never be a child again—her daddy's little girl. She felt the tears about to come, but she wouldn't allow them. "Why are you alone on your birthday?" she asked.

"The same as you," he answered. "People problems. My wife threw me out of the house two days ago and is filing for divorce. This is not the time for celebrating a birthday." He studied his glass for awhile, then drank the remaining drop and looked at the fire. "She had every right to do that. I haven't been a very attentive husband. I've spent every spare moment studying for the bar exam."

He got up and went over to the table, picked up the cupcake, then threw it into the fire. "So much for birthdays," he said. "So much for marriage." He looked at her then. "Maybe your boyfriend did you a favor."

She thought of his marriage—her mom and dad's— over! Suddenly another thought struck her. "You saved my life."

He shook his head. "You'd already turned when I got there." He paused. "Maybe you saved my life." He smiled. The first smile she'd seen since she came into the cottage. They stared at each other.

"My clothes might be dry," she said.

"I'll walk you back when the storm dies down," he said. "Or you're welcome to stay the night. You can take the bedroom. I don't sleep well these nights. Too much on my mind. But that's enough of my troubles."

Sharon stepped out of the afghan and stood as he turned to move away from the fire. His eyes swept over her, and he looked away. Sharon reached out and touched his arm. "I'm so sorry to burden you with my troubles. You have—"

"No," he interrupted. "Strangely it's been good for me, thinking about someone else's problems beside my own. I suppose it's kind of like your leaving the party. Sometimes you don't want to be around laughing, carefree people."

She never wanted to go back to that life awaiting her— a life without her family intact, without the security of the boyfriend she'd had for over a year.

"Happy birthday," she said and lifted her hands to touch

his face. She drew his head close to hers. Her lips touched his in a gentle kiss.

Who, or why, or how, had nothing to do with it, but she was lost in his kiss, in his arms that came around her in such swift, fierce intensity.

He pushed her away. "Angela," he said, "you don't know what you're doing."

"I do," she lied.

What followed had been wrong, of course, and desperately foolish. She'd slipped out the front door later that night after she was sure he was asleep and then made her way down the beach, in the light rain.

She knew she couldn't go home right away. Her mom would suspect. So she'd gone to her grandmother's house, a few blocks from the beach. Her grandmother was surprised, but accepted her explanation that she had left a dull party.

During that night of fitful sleep, Sharon remembered that she'd vowed never to speak to her father again. She'd said she hated his secretary. But now she, herself, had slept with an older man. She didn't even know the man. He might have been lying about getting a divorce, but even if he wasn't, how different was he from her own dad? *And I,* she thought shivering, *how different am I from my dad's secretary?*

&

Twenty-three years later, Sharon had forgiven herself and him. But she would never forget. That night in the beach house, her son, Robert, had been fathered by Marcus Sinclair.

six

Two days after Luke had called him, Marcus sat in his office with his mind wandering. He glanced at his watch at a little before three o'clock in the afternoon. Unable to concentrate on the murder-case files he'd been reading, he impatiently closed them, buzzed Ellen, his secretary, and said he was calling it a day.

Ellen had picked up an exact replica of the blood-soaked toy the previous day but had said that if it had been the little boy's favorite toy, it shouldn't look new, so she took it home to wash it. She was insightful like that. That was one thing that made her such a good secretary. A couple years earlier, the idea of settling down with Ellen, a comfortable widow in her late forties, had crossed Marcus's mind.

As he washed his hands in a courthouse bathroom, he realized those thoughts of settling down had gone down the drain, just like soapy water.

His reflection didn't even seem to mind. The man in the mirror was a happy man. After drying his hands, he ran his fingers through his thick dark hair that had silvered just enough to lend an air of distinction, so Ellen said.

Now Ellen was seeing someone else, and Marcus was enjoying his freedom.

Freedom? As a judge, a father, a man, he well knew the implication of such a word—not only from the U.S. Constitution, which gave the right not of happiness, but of the "pursuit"of it, but also from the realization that the Lord Himself offered not happiness but "abundant" life. *Ah, well, no time for philosophizing at the moment.*

Inhaling deeply, he choked on the thick odorous air, hurried from the small room, and continued on through the courthouse, toward the parking lot, smiling, speaking to colleagues with whom he'd had an enjoyable camaraderie for many years.

Once on the main road, he switched on his little red Thunderbird's radio, catching the three o'clock news. The same as last night—with an update on two-year-old Bobby Martin's condition. Still critical. The accident had been the talk of the courthouse yesterday and today.

Marcus didn't like hospitals. When his wife, Bev, died of cancer eight years ago, he'd gotten his fill of them. But he hadn't been able to shake Luke's entreaty for blood a couple of nights ago. And with his awareness that a little boy with the same blood type as one of his own grandsons needed his blood, he pulled into the hospital parking garage.

Oblivious to the warmth of the spring air and the rolling white clouds across an azure sky, Marcus chided himself that he, a grown man, should be apprehensive about giving blood. Yet he felt definitely squeamish by the time he reached Luke's office.

"You're white as a sheet, Dad," Luke said, the moment he stepped inside the office. "Better sit down. Giving blood can make you light-headed."

So much for appearing macho in front of Luke's pretty young assistant! "Hi, Julie."

Her radiant smile lit up her face like the light reflecting from her luxurious mane of medium-brown hair that was caught back in a twist. One errant strand accented the appealing flush of youth on her cheek. "Good to see you again, Judge Sinclair." Her voice softened. "Luke said you might be a donor."

Marcus knew the color he felt flush his own cheeks had nothing to do with youth. Reluctantly he admitted, "I haven't given blood yet."

"Mmmmm," Luke mumbled, with a knowing look in his eyes that he turned mischievously toward Julie.

Julie bent her head and looked condescendingly at Marcus, as one might a senile old man.

Acquiescing, Marcus lifted his hand. "I'm going to, pass out or not." Then he noticed the abundance of flowers and bags on the floors and on every flat surface. "What's all this?"

"For Bobby." Julie's eyes turned sympathetic. "The public is responding, but we can't have these in ICU."

Luke stood, his face serious. "He's still in a coma. Julie and I were just getting ready to check Bobby's vital signs. Would you like to see him?"

He wouldn't, but Marcus knew that Luke was taking a particularly personal interest in this case—as was the entire city, according to newspaper and TV reports.

Marcus looked at the little boy in a coma. That might be Luke's blood flowing from that IV into the little boy, keeping him alive. The boy was bruised, cut. Dark circles appeared beneath his closed eyes, where long dark lashes lay against his pale cheeks. On the white pillow lay a mop of reddish-golden brown hair, reminding him of the sun-touched hair of his own children when they were little, before their hair turned dark like his and Bev's.

Standing, watching Luke and Julie's quiet professional

teamwork, Marcus knew the little boy's life would mark them—had already. Trying to shake the depressing feeling of so young a life, so near death, he walked out into the hallway.

When Luke and Julie joined him, Luke said there was no change. Bobby was barely holding on.

Marcus held out the bag containing the dinosaur. "What shall I do with this?"

"Mrs. Martin went home to finalize arrangements for her mother's funeral that's scheduled for tomorrow morning. We plan to meet her in the cafeteria for an update after Julie and I finish our rounds. Why don't you join us and give it to her?"

Marcus wanted to get out of there but knew Luke and Julie couldn't very well make their rounds with a purple dinosaur.

Later, feeling better at having given his blood and praying it might be helpful to Bobby or another needy person, Marcus walked down the long corridor to the cafeteria. He did not go in, however, for he saw Luke and Julie at a table with a woman who lifted a tissue and wiped her eyes. But she also smiled and reached over to squeeze Luke's hand.

Feeling squeamish at the thought of hospital food, the giving of blood, the woman's losses, and the memory of the injured boy, Marcus decided this was no time for a social gathering. He left the hospital. Trying to assuage a stab of guilt, he told himself tomorrow would be a better time. He knew, from experience, that facing reality was more difficult after a funeral.

⧫

The following day, a warm spring morning, Sharon sat in

the swing on her mother's front porch, waiting for one of the kind neighbor couples who had offered to give her a ride to the church for her mother's funeral. She tried to assimilate all that had happened. However, she felt dazed, going through the motions like a zombie.

She needed to thank the Lord for Helen Gamble—for her help in arranging organ donations, and for her kind sympathy which extended beyond professionalism. And Beth had been a true friend.

Her mother's neighbors must have watched for the moment Sharon came home for something. They came bringing food, expressing their admiration and love for her mother, and showing their readiness to do anything necessary. They insisted Sharon eat and created pleasant memories of how helpful Earline Johnson had been in their times of need. Sharon was never alone during the day. At night she drifted in and out of sleep.

ৡ

"It was instant," Pastor Clark was saying as he delivered the eulogy.

Instant? Sharon thought. Maybe that's what made it so difficult to believe. They were there one instant—gone another. At times, she thought this was only a nightmare. She would awaken and her family would be there. But Pastor Clark was confirming they were in a better place.

Although the funeral was for Earline Johnson, he talked about Robert and Karen and how that as Christians they were with the Lord. Now the living must concentrate on and pray for Bobby—who had not yet awakened from his coma.

If I should die before I wake, settled upon Sharon's weary brain. Robert was only twenty-two. How awake was he?

Little more than a child himself. And now Bobby—only
two!

If I should die before I wake. . .

When Sharon had buried her husband five years before,
she still had her son. She could expect her dad, who lived
in Hawaii, to die someday, and her mother to die as well,
because that was the natural order of things. "We begin to
die the day we're born," she'd heard all her life. But it
was no comfort. . .no comfort.

Even when she had to make the decision that her son
and his wife would be flown to California to await decisions about their burial, even as she sat at her mother's
funeral, the primary thought, the one reason to be not
strong, not courageous, not brave—she was none of
that—but just to hang on, was Bobby.

The prayer she prayed as a child kept echoing in her
mind, even as the preacher extolled the attributes of her
mother:

> *If I should die before I wake*
> *I pray the Lord my soul to take.*

Children weren't taught that prayer anymore. Parents
thought it was too scary, too morbid. She had never
thought of the morbidity of the prayer, only that she
should have her heart right with God, should death happen. Now the thought touched her heart like an abscessed
tooth, or a fingernail chewed to the quick.

Oh, God, don't let Bobby die before he wakes.

In her bereft, shocked world there was no longer reality.
Instead she stood in a place of waiting, as if she were on
the shore waiting for the storm to come. She'd seen it.

The storm clouds gather, hover, press down, the winds blow the palm fronds. She'd felt it on her face.

If I should die before I wake. Don't take him. He's all I've got. Oh, Lord, don't take him. I need him. My son is in him. I would be left with nothing—just. . .bereft. Yes, I know I will have my memories, my years of blessings. I've had a good life. Some people never do. I am grateful. I have thanked You. But Bobby is only two. He has not begun to live. No, that's not why. I want him for myself. I want that grandchild. For me. To give me a reason to live.

If he should die before he wakes then my life would be empty—like a motel with a flashing neon sign: VACANCY . . .VACANCY. . .VACANCY.

৯

Later that day, Nancy Clark drove Sharon to the hospital. Sharon would be staying there as much as possible now that her mother was buried. She needed to be near Bobby, and even near Dr. Luke, the half-brother her son had never known he had.

She could not allow herself to break down. Later, she could cry, she could grieve. She could feel that vacancy sign hitting against her ribs, thudding against her chest. The heat of it burned her stomach. The tears constricted her throat. But it mustn't come yet.

Sharon had not been in Charleston several years before when Hurricane Hugo hit the coastline with gale force winds of 150 miles per hour, unleashing its fury, wreaking havoc, destroying homes, ruining businesses, taking lives. But she had seen the devastation on TV, had read the accounts in the newspaper. She remembered the nationally televised comments: "It's unbelievable. I've lost everything. I don't know what to do. I've been in hurricanes before, but never anything like this."

That's how Sharon felt. Three days before, her personal hurricane had struck. On a rain-slick highway, a tractor-trailer lost control and slammed into the car carrying her mother, her son, his wife, and her two-year-old grandson. She'd known tragedy, disaster, personal loss. But never anything like this.

But she had one chance for survival. Little Bobby was her lifeboat. She was clinging to the side—knowing all the while that in a storm like this, even a ship could sink.

She'd handled it well after her husband died five years before. But this was different. Robert was her son—her only son, her child, her baby who had grown inside her. He had been her reason for living. All that was gone. . . gone.

Spurred by sheer determination, Sharon strode purposefully down the somber hospital corridor, willing the walls not to close in on her. Bobby mustn't die. He was all she had. Head set, shoulders squared, emotions suppressed, she kept her mind's eye focused on her mission, and her light blue gaze on the door at the far end.

She pressed a button on the wall, and the doors to ICU opened. An unusual amount of movement stirred at Bobby's doorway, and she saw cleaning ladies with their carts. Hurrying to his room, she had to grasp the glass door to keep from falling. She couldn't speak, couldn't feel, was afraid to think.

Her breath came in short spurts.

The room was empty.

Bobby was gone.

seven

The corridor of the pediatric ward looked like a fantasyland with pink and blue castles, trees with tender green and yellow leaves, and a profusion of wildflowers in various shapes, sizes, and colors through which animals of every sort ran freely. Little people, nymphs, and elves roamed the forest, crossed bridges over sparkling streams, and danced in circles while holding hands. All of that, beneath a blue sky dotted fluffy white clouds and a big smiling yellow sun.

Passing rooms with open doors, Sharon saw that children were in rooms that had walls painted different colors. Smiling, happy nurses wore pink, purple, and light blue outfits, on which were boldly printed figures of animals.

Sesame Street characters ran across the bottom of the nurses' station. Sharon couldn't help but smile. Everything in this ward was so upbeat, so colorful, and would appeal to children.

Helen Gamble led Sharon into a room where Luke and Julie stood on each side of Bobby's bed, raising the rails, giving the appearance of a crib. That was good. They thought he was well enough that he might roll. Sharon looked from Luke to Julie, both smiling.

"He's coming out of the coma," Luke explained. "His eyes have fluttered open, and he's made faint sounds. He could awaken at any time."

"It's best that he awaken in a room like this," Julie added.

Sharon had not been able to take her eyes off Bobby. He was still hooked up to IVs and a catheter to drain his bladder.

"The soft restraints on his wrists," Julie explained, "are so he won't inadvertently pull out his IVs when he wakes up."

Sharon nodded. That meant they expected him to be well and active before long. He did look better. More color in his face. His bruises were darker, surrounded by a sickly yellow cast, but that was part of healing. Much of the swelling had gone down. After a moment, Julie's remark registered. Sharon looked around, seeing that colorful fish swam on a border around the middle of the light blue walls. There was another bed in the room—for her.

"Yes," she said. "It's a wonderful room."

Her eyes returned to Bobby. "Can he hear us?"

"That seems to be an individual thing," Luke said. "Many have claimed to know what was going on while they were unconscious or coming out of it. Others have known nothing. But we are keeping him sedated to alleviate any pain." Luke motioned for Sharon to come closer.

The urge to grasp Bobby in her arms and hold him close, never let him go, was overpowering. But Sharon had to merely reach out and let her fingers gently touch a place on his little face that wasn't bruised. Her finger traced a pattern around one ear. Her hand lay gently over his little heart, that beat steadily. . .with life.

She drew back, lest he feel her emotion. Since the accident, her tears had been drops of grief. She could not, would not, hold back these tears of relief. Bobby would recover.

Helen handed her a tissue. Sharon wiped her eyes and smiled.

Luke put his arm around her shoulders—like her son

would have done, had he lived. How right it seemed, having her son's half-brother comfort her.

A smiling nurse came in, wearing an outfit with colorful teddy bears all over it. She introduced herself as Meg, Bobby's nurse until 11:00 P.M. Luke asked Sharon to step out into the hallway with him.

"We have every reason to believe Bobby will recover physically. But we can't know just yet what problems may have been caused by the head trauma. It's out of our hands now. But we can pray."

"Oh, yes," Sharon said, returning his smile. She was grateful for all these wonderful people who had been lifesavers for her—and Bobby.

She glanced down the hall as Luke and Julie walked away. His hand touched the small of Julie's back. The way his young assistant looked up at him gave Sharon the impression Julie greatly admired Dr. Luke. They obviously made a great team.

Helen Gamble walked from the nurse's station with a huge teddy bear. Beside her was an L.P.N. bearing a pot of coffee and cups.

"You're so thoughtful, Helen," Sharon said.

"Well, I knew you wouldn't budge from this room anytime soon. Besides, I need to discuss this with you."

Sharon stared. She wasn't surprised that Helen might bring Bobby a bear, but this one was old and worn, with a missing eye. And the look in Helen's eye indicated something serious was afoot.

❧

Luke and Julie walked to the nurses' station and went into a back office where they could discuss their cases. It was Luke's responsibility to train Julie. She was into her first

year of the three years of residency required and was glad
to have him as her supervisor. He had the reputation of
sending out his residents as highly equipped M.D.s. On
more than one occasion he'd recommended a resident
train for longer than three years. Lives hung in the balance. Working with him was an inspiration. Besides that,
they had wonderful conversations about art and music.

Julie came from a family of doctors and strove to be as
good as they had been. Lately, however, she felt like a
tightrope about to snap. She'd been on the floor before
6:30 that morning, made rounds with Luke, then met with
the attending physicians in the conference room on the
Peds floor. They'd discussed patients' status, treatment
plans, and expected the attending physicians' input.

She knew she wasn't the only one on such a schedule.
The other residents were as exhausted as she, and they
understood the doctors had all gone through the same
thing. Julie was determined to make it. The morning wore
on, and she wrote orders and progress notes, checked lab
work, and talked with nurses and the families of patients.

By lunchtime, Julie went up to the suite of rooms set
aside for the attending physicians. They shared a kitchen
and bathroom, but each had a private bedroom. Julie went
into her room and locked the door. She opened the top
drawer of her bedside table and took out the bottle of pills.
She sat on the bed, resisting the urge to crawl under the
covers and sleep for hours. For a moment she considered
the little pill bottle bearing the name of Amy Smith. It con-
tained a prescription of Prozac from Dr. Julie Dalton.

Her family doctor had prescribed the antidepressant
Prozac while Julie was in medical school. She certainly
wasn't the only med student who needed medication.

There had been many reasons then to be depressed, not only with the demands of med school but with the loss of her boyfriend who couldn't wait for her.

Now she needed an occasional stimulant, and this was one of those times. She had had two hours of sleep last night, at the most. Bobby's case was taking up so much time. Another child with respiratory distress had to be incubated and placed on a ventilator.

These are not excuses, Julie reminded herself, forcing herself to rise from the bed and pour water from the pitcher on the dresser. She had reasons to get through this trying time. Luke was one of them. She couldn't chance making a bad impression on him. She quickly took the pill and rejoined life on the floor.

By the end of the afternoon, Julie desperately needed sleep but felt so wired she knew it wouldn't come. This was more difficult than med school. The hours were so long. She had decisions to make and had to be alert.

She was about to head for her room when an R.N. approached her with a chart. "Late last night Kaitlain woke up, complaining that her leg hurt. Then she didn't wake up again until noon. I'm concerned that her pain medication may be too strong."

"Let me see," Julie said and pondered over the chart. "Kaitlain had a longer physical therapy session yesterday than usual. That could have caused soreness in the muscles. I'll take a look at her. Here," she said, holding out her hands. "Let me take the medication in."

Walking toward the room, she heard the R.N. telling one of the other nurses, "Julie is so sweet and more dedicated than any doctor I know."

How could I be less dedicated? My entire family has

been in some field of medicine. These little children need me. She realized, however, that Bobby's situation had taken its toll on her—emotionally and physically. But she would not be able to rest tonight if she didn't see Kaitlain.

Eleven-year-old Kaitlain was sitting up in bed, laughing while watching the Disney Channel. She glanced and groaned upon seeing Julie. Julie laughed. "Don't mind me. I just want to take a look at that leg." She set the tray on the bedside table.

Kaitlain paid little attention to Julie's probing hands and gentle massage of her calf that had been pulled severely in a skating accident when she'd fallen and another skater had fallen on top of her. At one point, Kaitlain said, "Ouch!"

At Julie's questioning, Kaitlain revealed the leg felt better than it had previously. Today's therapy had seemed to take some of the soreness away.

"I understand you woke up with pain last night," Julie said.

"Yeah, but it feels better now than it has before."

"Great! That's how it's supposed to be."

Kaitlain returned her smile, then again focused on the TV.

Julie stepped over to the medication, turned the little cup upside down in her hand and looked at the two pills. One was a children's Tylenol. The other, a stronger pain medication. She returned the Tylenol to the cup and slipped the other pill into her pocket.

"Take your medication," Julie gently instructed, holding out the cup and water. Kaitlain didn't ask why her medication had changed from two pills to one. She downed the Tylenol and returned her attention to the TV.

Julie returned the water cup to the table. "Glad you're

feeling better. Keep on like this, and you'll be out of here before you know it."

Kaitlain grimaced. "No way! I'd have to go back to school."

They laughed, just as the supper tray was brought in.

"There'd better be ice cream on that tray," the girl said.

"Sorry," the woman said.

Kaitlain patted Julie's shoulder. "I'll see that you get ice cream."

Kaitlain smiled up at her. The woman smiled too, with a sidelong look that said Julie would spoil these children.

At the nurse's station, Julie dropped off the chart, ordered ice cream for Kaitlain, and said she was going to her room. They would call her if they needed her.

Just this once, Julie told herself. And it wasn't as if she were taking anything away from Kaitlain that she needed. This was a mild pain medication for an adult, just enough to take the edge off and help her sleep.

Her hand was in her pocket and a smile was on her face as she rode the elevator up to her room. She felt better already, knowing that sleep was ahead of her—in the form of a little pill.

eight

The following morning, Sharon was kneeling on the carpeted floor of the children's recreation room, loading a miniature school bus with little block people, counting as she loaded, which was a type of therapy for the little girl who'd had a head injury and had to relearn everything. Professionals were in charge, but Sharon had volunteered to help, at least for an hour or so each day. She was so grateful to all who were helping Bobby. She had to try to reciprocate in some way.

She had slept several hours last night, having lain in the bed just a few feet away from Bobby. During the evening she had talked to him, touched him, even turned the TV on for a brief period, coming to the realization that there was a world outside this hospital. She had been aware of nurses coming in through the night to check on Bobby and heard them whisper softly, "He's doing just fine."

Then early this morning, Julie had come in, with her bright sparkling smile and exuberant spirit. She confirmed that Bobby was resting well while his little body healed. "A breakfast tray is being brought up for you, Sharon," Julie said. "My orders are that you eat it."

Sharon promised. She couldn't help but respond to such a lovely, caring young woman.

"Mrs. Martin?" came the soft voice of Suzie, a young L.P.N. who appeared in the doorway of the recreation room. Suzie seemed to attend to Sharon's needs almost as much as she did the children's. Sharon felt a particular fondness for the young girl who believed her nursing career was God's mission for her life. "There's a man here to see you."

"A man?" Suzie would have named a doctor. Perhaps someone from an insurance company—business as usual, even if the losses had not completely struck her yet. Then Suzie's words caught her completely off guard.

"Not just any man," Suzie said, smiling. "It's Judge Sinclair. Dr. Luke's dad."

Never had Sharon been more grateful for a child's wail than when Suzie bent down to load the bus for Maria. Sharon felt paralyzed—more helpless than the children in wheelchairs. The emotional paralysis prevented her moving, prevented her breathing. She wasn't ready for this. She would never be ready for this. Was he. . .outside, looking through the window at her? Would he wonder why she was on her knees even now when no child was near her?

Willing herself to move, Sharon rose to her feet and brushed at the knees of her pants as if the carpet had left some sort of stain on them. She stared at the closed door. Ready! Was she really ready? She told her heart to be reasonable and forced her mind to think calmly.

Robotlike, she opened the door and stepped out into the waiting area. He was not there, but beyond, in the hallway, conversing with a nurse at the station. Her eyes moved to the corner of the waiting room and studied the table on which a glass coffeepot sat, half empty. Near it was a stack of foam cups, plastic spoons, napkins, and a small bowl of pink-and-white paper packages. She wouldn't be able to hold a cup of coffee without spilling it. She must sit before she collapsed. But when he walked in, she'd have to stand out of politeness. Would she be able to? Maybe she could walk out to the nurses' station and lean against the partition.

She tried. But a nurse glanced in her direction, and he turned.

Sharon was bone-weary and mind-numb. She'd done some hard things in her life, but this was among the hardest.

She knew she had to be the first to speak. Just the thought of hearing his voice sent her emotions spiraling into the past. *This is the father of my beloved son—the grandfather of little Bobby.*

She hoped she was prepared to hear his voice, but when he questioned, "Mrs. Martin?" she felt as if someone had jabbed her in the sides. She started, swayed slightly, stopped, and held onto the door casing for balance. She drew in her breath. She would know him anywhere.

She had subscribed to the *Charleston Times* and saved newspaper articles and announcements about Marcus in case Robert ever wanted to know about his birth father. She learned that Marcus had not divorced when she read his wife had her third child, a boy now in college. She knew when Luke married, when Marcus's only daughter Kathleen married, when Luke got a scholarship to college. She knew when Marcus and his wife went on a trip to the Holy Land with a church group, and Sharon believed he had found peace within himself since that night so long ago when he was as troubled as she. She knew when he was appointed to the bench, and when his wife died of cancer eight years ago. She'd seen him on TV, in the newspapers, in the face of her son—the son who had lived, and died, without Marcus ever knowing of his existence.

Sharon was sure he wouldn't remember her. She had changed since she was nineteen. Her hair was short now, a softer shade of brown. She was twenty pounds heavier and had replaced her southern accent with a California brogue. Why would he remember her from one night in all of his fifty-one years? He wouldn't want to remember.

He was looking at her like he had twenty-three years ago, with that same expression of inquisitive kindness. She mustn't call him Marcus. She mustn't extend her hand for him to touch. She mustn't say, "Let's talk about our son, Robert, and grieve together."

His face began to swim before her eyes, and she took a deep breath, reminding herself that life was now about Bobby—only Bobby.

"Judge Sinclair," she said, repeating his words after he introduced himself. But still she did not extend her hand. She must not let go of the door casing, the only thing allowing her to stay on her feet.

What was he seeing as he looked at her? Her soft brown hair was swept back on one side and fell along her face on the other to just below her jawline. She wore casual, yet stylish gray slacks with matching jacket over a cream-colored silk blouse. She knew her blue eyes would reveal her grief, but she tried to mask any emotion.

It seemed an eternity to Sharon before he said in the voice she remembered, "Could we sit and talk for a moment?"

That meant she'd have to let go of the door casing. She'd have to turn. But at least she could sit. His hand was outstretched in a gesture toward the waiting room. Automatically she followed his motion, physically let go of the door casing, turned, and found a chair. He was a blur as he came into the room and she barely registered his dark blue suit. She was seeing him at that other time, before his hair turned to silver at the temples, when he was leaner, at a time when he wondered what life had in store for him. He'd done well. So well.

His quick steps across the multicolored carpet took him to the couch across from her. Spry, for a man of fifty-one. She knew his age. She knew his birthday. She wanted to say, "You've done well, Marcus." But she couldn't— mustn't.

He started to sit, then paused. His look was curious. "Would you like to sit, Mrs. Martin?"

She sat.

"Luke, my son, the doctor," he began, and Sharon nodded, still unable to meet his eyes. "He told me about the accident and has taken a personal interest in Bobby."

Sharon's smile was faint. She must concentrate on Bobby. Only Bobby. She nodded.

The judge took a Barney dinosaur from a bag that hadn't really registered with Sharon until now.

"Oh, it's Bobby's. Or like it."

"My secretary washed it to give it a worn look."

Sharon reached for it. "This is so good of you to do this. It will mean a lot to Bobby." She looked it over. There had been a worn patch on the left ear where the dog had roughed it up. But it was like the one Bobby had. Marcus must have seen it. It must have been in bad shape.

Bobby's grandfather was bringing him a toy—just like his favorite animal. It seemed so right. And yet, Marcus didn't know—must never know. Her eyes closed against the thought.

"I have donated my blood, Mrs. Martin," he was saying. "I have the same type as Bobby."

She looked down at the dinosaur and was grateful for something to hold on to. She willed her fingers not to squeeze so fiercely. "Thank you," she whispered. "So much."

"If there's anything I can do. . ." he began.

She shrank back into the back of the chair when he leaned forward, his elbows resting on his thighs. "In the meantime," he said, "I'll. . .pray."

Pray? Her eyes met his and held for a long moment, before hers began to swim and she closed them as the liquid bathed her cheeks.

"You do know the Lord will give you strength for this?" he questioned.

"Oh, yes," she replied. "Please pray."

He bowed his head and began to pray—for her, for Bobby, for God's will. Sharon was so surprised she did not even close her eyes. She simply stared at the man who did not wait until some more convenient, more private time to pray. He prayed openly, sincerely.

When he said, "Amen," Sharon echoed the word, then asked, "Would you like to see Bobby?"

৯

Marcus's heart went out to the tiny, gaunt figure against the white sheets as Sharon told him how Bobby had awakened last evening and appeared to recognize her, and had even smiled before drifting off again into that realm where his little body was in the process of healing itself. She repeated what Luke had told Marcus, that the body would heal, but they didn't know yet about the little boy's swollen brain.

Trying to shake the depressing feeling of seeing a life so young lie so near death, Marcus looked around the room. His gaze fell upon a big stuffed brown bear on a side table. It looked almost as big as the child and about as abused, with worn spots, a missing eye, and an ear that had been hand-stitched back on. "The bear must be another of the little fellow's toys," Marcus commented.

"No," Sharon replied, as she took the dinosaur over and sat it beside the bear. "It belonged to the teenage boy who received an organ donation from Bobby's dad. It was his favorite, and he'd kept it through the years. He wanted Bobby to have it."

Marcus stared blurry-eyed at the bear, absorbing this new information. What an exchange—and yet, it was the best the teenager had to offer. The bear sat staring expressionless with that one beady eye, as if watching over the child.

But what could a bear do? A memory flashed. Marcus saw his grandmother's wall. A faded picture of Jesus watching over a boy and a girl on a dilapidated old foot bridge. *Surely, Lord, You'll watch over this little guy? What is best? I can't know. Your will be done. But look down on this little one.*

Marcus's eyes then fell upon a picture in a small frame sitting beside the bear. He walked over and picked it up. A young man and woman were sitting and a little boy perched on the man's knee. So much like the studio pictures Luke's family had made once a year. This must be little Bobby. The inverted-bowl haircut, with bangs straight across the forehead, was like that of so many little boys, including his own grandsons.

If the little boy regained consciousness, he'd awaken to a picture—not parents. They were gone. His great-grandmother was gone. At least, he had a grandmother.

But what would all this do to the lifeless figure lying in that bed? And to this grandmother?

Marcus shuddered, and lest it be noticed by Sharon, he sat down in a nearby chair, even before Sharon sat on the edge of the extra bed in the room. She gestured to the many boxes stacked against the wall. "From the public," she said in awe. "I never knew strangers could be so caring."

"Strangers are caring. And here, I'm the attending physician's dad. How can I leave here with having only made that general remark of letting me know if I can do anything? Do you need transportation?" he asked. Luke had said she'd stayed at her mother's home until Bobby left ICU. "I'm free to drive you anywhere you need to go or pick up anything for you."

"I'm fine, thank you," Sharon answered. Helen had become a friend Sharon wouldn't mind asking a favor of when she wasn't working. Also the pastor and his wife were available, as well as neighbors. Then there were always taxicabs.

Marcus stood. "When you're ready, Mrs. Martin, I can give legal advice, help with any decisions. Please feel free to call on me. I mean it." He reached inside his suit coat and drew out a business card.

Sharon took it, although she didn't need it to know how to reach him. She rose from the bed. "My mother's attorney has already been in touch with me. I think that will be sufficient, Judge Sinclair."

"Marcus," he corrected, and she looked down from his smile, his caring eyes, the warmth in his voice.

"Thank you," she murmured.

❧

When he left the room, Sharon stood motionless. Only for

an instant could she allow herself to admire the man
Marcus had become—a man of God, a family man who
had reared successful children and with whom Luke obviously had a close relationship. A man more personally
appealing than that troubled young man of twenty-three
years ago.

Sharon pictured Marcus walking down the hall, into the
elevator with the doors slowly closing, until he disappeared altogether.

Like the elevator door, her mind must close on the past.
She would have no further contact with Marcus Sinclair.

nine

Two days later, Marcus appeared at the doorway of Bobby's room. Luke had kept him posted on Bobby's condition and on Sharon, who had become like a member of the pediatric-floor family and insisted upon being called by her first name.

Luke said she was responding to every piece of mail that had a return address and that the money sent to her—a considerable amount—was being donated to the pediatric ward. Besides helping with the care of Bobby, she volunteered a couple hours a day in the play room.

Luke apparently considered her an exceptional woman, one to be greatly admired. Marcus, himself, had been drawn to her. It was not just sympathy because she had lost three loved ones in an instant. Nor the fact that she was an attractive woman. He had prayed aloud in her presence, for her and Bobby. Something about praying for a person formed a bond—made it personal—and he thought of her not as Mrs. Martin but as Sharon.

He stepped inside the room, holding a stack of books. When Sharon looked up, surprised, her face paled. Then he became aware that a couple sat on the edge of her bed.

He held out the books. "My grandchildren wanted to give these to Bobby. Three-year-old Mark said if you read this one to Bobby, he will wake up and laugh."

"Thank you, Judge Sinclair," she said, and her eyes flew to his and held a moment. "I mean. . .Marcus," she corrected. His dark eyes gleamed with pleasure.

"I won't intrude," he said, taking a step backward after Sharon took the books.

"Wait." Sharon laid the books on the table by Bobby's bed. "I'd like to introduce you to Bobby's maternal grandparents. They flew in this morning from California."

The couple stood. "Mary and James Davis. Judge Marcus Sinclair."

Marcus extended his hand to James. "I'm so sorry about your losses," he said, looking from James to Mary. He tried to convey his empathy with their situation. "If there is any way I can be of assistance to you, please don't hesitate to ask."

Seeing the questioning look in Mary's and James's eyes, Sharon said quickly, as if having to explain, "You met Dr. Luke Sinclair. Judge Sinclair is his father. They both have been so kind." She turned to look at the children's books.

"A judge?" James questioned.

"Municipal court," Marcus replied, feeling uncomfortable. At a time like this, Sharon Martin shouldn't have to explain him. She had enough problems. He, too, saw the inquisitive look in the couple's eyes and the way Sharon had turned to look at the books as if she were embarrassed.

"Nice to meet you," he said. "My prayers are with you. Is there anything I can do? Bring something for you? Take you out to dinner?"

"Thanks," James said, "But we're on California time and had a bite not long ago."

"We've been trying to get Sharon to at least go to the cafeteria," Mary added. "It's my understanding she hasn't left here in days."

"At least come down and have a cup of coffee, Sharon," Marcus offered.

She concentrated on inspecting the books. Finally she turned, looking at the couple. "I've learned where all the coffee stations are. And my supper is always sent up to me, as if I were a patient." Her smile softened her face. "But I could run home for a few items."

"I'll be glad to drive you," Marcus offered.

"No, that's all right," Sharon said.

"You have a ride?" he asked.

"Not really," she hedged. "Perhaps I could take the rental car?" She looked from Mary to James.

"I believe that's against the law," Marcus said seriously, but a grin played about his mouth.

James laughed. "The insurance only covers Mary and me. And with a judge standing here, I'd say you might get arrested if you drove it."

"I'm on the verge of reading her Miranda Rights," Marcus said, and they all laughed lightly.

Sharon smiled.

"Please," Marcus said.

Sharon nodded her agreement.

Marcus sensed that she felt they'd ganged up on her and she mustn't make a scene.

Mary added, "You can sleep at home tonight, Sharon, if you want. I can stay here. James can stay here or with you, whatever you like."

"No, no," Sharon said quickly. "I'll come right back. I . . . I need to stay here."

"All right, Sharon," Mary replied. "Whatever you want. Now, you scoot. Everything will be fine here."

Sharon nodded. "I'll be back soon, sweet baby." She

kissed her fingers, laid them gently on Bobby's cheek, then walked out into the hallway with Marcus Sinclair.

Marcus smiled to himself. A small victory had just been won.

೩

"Oh, I'd better give you directions to Mount Pleasant," Sharon said, when Marcus pulled out of the parking garage onto a main road.

"Mount Pleasant," he repeated. "I believe I can find it without any trouble."

Of course he could, she told herself. It was a suburb of Charleston. He had lived in the area all of his life. He would know it better than she.

Maybe it was simply saying the name of the quiet section, "Mount Pleasant," aloud, but she felt more relaxed than she had since the accident. It was so reassuring to not have to go through all this alone. Strangers cared, friends helped, Bobby's maternal grandparents were here, and her fear of Marcus recognizing her had been unfounded. This drive would become a part of her memories—the better ones.

Her eyes lifted. The sun had disappeared, leaving behind a serene, cloudless sky. If only it had been clear last week. If only the spring storm hadn't come on so suddenly or so violently. If only they had planned their annual trip for later in the year.

"Relatives," Marcus was saying, drawing her back to the present. "Do you have any close by? To be with you?"

"No," she said quietly and looked at her hands clutching her purse. "But Mother has neighbors who are willing to do anything."

She looked over at him helplessly. "It's just that there's not much anyone can do."

Marcus nodded with understanding.

"For several years now, I've come to Charleston during the Spoleto Festival and sometimes for holidays. This is the first year Robert, Karen, and Bobby flew down with me." She took a deep breath. "Mitchell used to come with me."

"Mitchell?" he questioned.

A forlorn smile touched Sharon's lips. "My husband." She liked talking about Mitchell, the man she had married when Robert was five years old. Mitchell had raised him, loved him as if he were his own son. "He treated me like a queen," she said. "He died of a heart attack five years ago."

Marcus frowned. "That must have been a shock."

Sharon nodded. "His family had a history of heart disease. But he took care of himself and had shown no signs of trouble. He lived longer than many members of his family with the same problem. He was sixty-one."

"Sixty-one?" Marcus questioned, wondering if he'd heard correctly.

"He was older than I."

Marcus smiled. "I would never have believed you were sixty-one anyway."

"I'm forty-three," she said. *No longer a naive nineteen-year-old.*

Marcus turned on the car lights. Others were being turned on, one by one, like yellow eyes, glowing in the twilight. Like the years of her life, they came close, then whizzed by, only to be followed by another. Life was like that. Yesterday she was nineteen—today she was forty-three. It came—and went—so swiftly. All the chances worth taking came only once.

A ray of late afternoon sun penetrated the windshield and sparked Marcus's dark brown eyes with golden flecks. It touched his hair, not tousled brown anymore, but laced with silver and cut conservatively short. He was as handsome now if not more so, with a fuller, more mature face. The lines around his mouth and at his eyes were deeper, giving character.

She knew he could empathize with her, having experienced personal loss himself. And at times like this, there really wasn't anything else to talk about. "You've lost someone," she said, rather than asked.

He turned onto a main street, leaving the sunshine behind them. "My wife died of cancer three years ago," he said. "She lived only four months after it was discovered. We were glad she didn't have to suffer long."

"It's always hard on children," Sharon said, wondering how Bobby would deal with this. Her eyes closed, and her head felt like lead on her shoulders.

"They're more resilient than we often give them credit for," Marcus continued, as if knowing she thought of Bobby. "One of our sons was a teenager. Luke and our daughter were already married when Bev died. That helps, I think."

"When Mitchell died of a heart attack, Robert was in college. Robert. . ." Her voice broke. "Robert is my son. The only child I could ever have."

My son, my son! her mind screamed, and it made her throat and head ache. *Our son, Marcus.* She took a tissue from her purse and turned her head toward the window.

"You have Bobby. You have your memories." He added desolately, "That doesn't help, does it?"

"It does help. My world has ended several times during

my forty-three years of life. But I've had many wonderful beginnings, too. I have been greatly blessed, and I know this is the darkest time of my life. It's something I have to go through. There are no shortcuts through my grief. I know there is pain before there is healing. Although I may seem unable to cope. . ." She drew in a breath. "I am an optimist."

She lifted her shimmering blue eyes and met his sympathetic gaze.

"You'll make it, Sharon," he said with confidence. "You're a strong woman."

"Oh," she said suddenly, "You missed the turn-off."

"I know a different way. Just sit still and leave the driving to me," he said, and the sound of his voice held a playful intimacy that fluttered over her like a butterfly over flowers, fanning possibility. The thought both thrilled and frightened her.

Her eyes shut tightly against the intrusion of the thought of a man in her life. She had reconciled herself to the fact that there would never be another one after Mitchell.

"They lived with me," she said quickly, too quickly, but felt it imperative to dispel her mind's foolish ramblings. "Robert, Karen, and Bobby. Robert was studying architecture. Mitchell was a builder."

"I suppose his dad influenced that decision," Marcus said, watching the traffic carefully.

"Robert respected him so much." She did not reveal that she had been the receptionist in Mitchell's company until they married. "Karen—that's Robert's wife—she worked as an executive secretary for a businessman. Very efficient young woman."

She smiled over at Marcus. "Later on, I became Bobby's

full-time baby-sitting grandmother." She laughed lightly. "Except there wasn't much sitting involved."

Marcus gave a short laugh. "I understand. I have three grandchildren of my own."

There was a pause as Marcus turned onto a road leading to the Cooper River Bridge. "Since your husband died, you've had no life of your own?"

"My family was my life."

He gave her a long look as his head turned toward the right, the direction in which the car turned.

Sharon felt she had not answered his question.

Marcus knew she had.

৵

The first thing Sharon did when she and Marcus arrived at her mother's house was to call the hospital, letting Mary know they had arrived. Mary reported that all was fine.

As soon as Sharon hung up, a neighbor called, asking if she'd had supper.

"No, but—"

"How many are there?"

"Two, but we—"

"I'll be right over."

Several minutes later an elderly woman and man parked behind Marcus's car, and each brought in a plate covered with foil. "Earline and I often exchanged recipes," she said. "This is her favorite meat loaf. I hope you'll like it."

Sharon couldn't refuse this kind offer. They left after repeating, "Let us know if we can do anything."

"I planned to take you out to a restaurant," Marcus began, but Sharon was shaking her head.

"That takes too long. I need to get back to the hospital soon." She removed the foil to see two plates filled with meat loaf, mashed potatoes, and broccoli. She didn't know if she could sit and have small talk with Marcus. After getting silverware, she said, "Tell me about your children."

He proudly spoke of his daughter Kathleen, expecting her first child, and living on the other side of Charleston. His son Grant was a senior at the Citadel.

The informal meal was soon over, and Marcus suggested he review Earline Johnson's legal papers while Sharon arranged the house for Mary and James's stay that night.

On the ride back to the hospital, Marcus explained that her mother's will left everything to Sharon, which she already knew. The house was paid for, and there was a small insurance policy. Her mother's car was new, since her mother preferred to trade every two years to prevent having to deal with repairs.

"You'll need to notify the Social Security Administration and Medicare of her death," Marcus advised.

Sharon was so grateful for Marcus's help. She'd had to do many of the things he advised after Mitchell died. But she'd had Robert with her then. They had helped each other get through it.

"Luke said Bobby will take several months to return to health, so I'll turn mother's bedroom into a room for him."

"I may be able to help out with some things," Marcus said. "Mark has only recently outgrown his high chair, and it's in Luke's basement. Seems like there's a youth bed. I'll check."

"I can't let you keep helping me like this, Marcus," Sharon protested.

"Why not?" he asked, with a sidelong glance and a grin.

Of course, she couldn't tell him.

Just then they reached the front of the hospital, where Marcus dropped her off. Sharon hurried to Bobby's hospital room, but she felt as if the short time spent with Marcus had been a bright spot in this tragic situation. Sitting in the passenger seat, having a man drive her somewhere, was something she now realized she'd missed since Mitchell's death. She liked being independent, but she also liked having a man do things for her—with her.

She had faith that some good always came from the worst of things. She'd seen it happen time and again in her own life. And now, good was happening again. Bobby's relatives were near him, caring about him. Her mother, her son, and his wife were in heaven. Sharon would raise Bobby. She'd already had a good start, having been his primary caregiver from the time he was born. He would recover. They'd be a family.

Yes, she had much to look forward to. She was eager to tell Mary and James her plans for Bobby.

Shortly after going into Bobby's room and seeing that he was asleep, Sharon sat on her bed beside Mary and looked over at James in the chair.

"I've been making plans for Bobby," she said with the first trace of excitement she'd felt in a long time. "I want to get legal custody of him," she said, knowing he belonged to her in every way that mattered except as his legal parent.

"Sharon," James said seriously, while Mary looked down at the floor. "Mary and I have been discussing that very thing."

Mary looked up. Although her eyes were sad, her words were clear. "We think it best if James and I have custody of Bobby."

ten

Kaitlain's pain pill helped Julie through a rough time—and with no apparent adverse effects. After her first decent few hours of sleep in days, she'd checked the records. Kaitlain had slept, so Julie discussed the dosage with Luke and they reduced the level of the pain medication.

While Luke complimented Julie on her sensitivity to Kaitlain's needs, Julie rationalized that what she'd done had turned out even better for Kaitlain and herself. However, she felt so guilty, she vowed never, ever again to chance putting a child in jeopardy. Luke's trust in her must not be harmed, nor the children's, nor for that matter, her own trust in herself.

She sailed through the morning like a new person, while Luke's face bore a perpetual smile. They exchanged a few jokes, lunched together, and he even asked her opinion about a particularly difficult case.

Julie stopped by Luke's office before leaving for the day. Several of the residents on the day shift for the week-end had decided to eat out and take in a movie.

"Want to join us?" Julie asked. She was wearing a sunny yellow dress that matched both her personality and the bright spring day.

Luke laughed and lifted his hand in a farewell gesture to the spirited young woman.

&

After two days of eight-hour shifts, Julie went on twenty-four-hour call. She felt ready for it. Until the school bus accident. She'd never been so shaken as when she saw those small mangled children. But the little girl that Dr. Thomas, Luke, and she worked on all evening and into the night was going to be all right. She had to be.

They worked for hours, unaware of fatigue, only of having to save the child's life. After hours and hours of surgery and working with the child, the heart stopped. Julie administered resuscitation, but it didn't work. She willed the child to breathe, demanded the little girl's heart start beating.

The heart remained stubbornly still.

The child didn't take another breath.

The little girl was dead.

Luke held Julie while she cried. "I've never lost a patient before," she wailed.

"That's the worse part," Luke said. The two took comfort from each other. They had shared the most dreaded experience in medicine.

"Now, we have to tell the parents," he said.

Julie looked up at him. "Oh, I can't possibly." That was the hardest. One never learned to be totally objective. Saving lives was their top priority. In this case, they had been helpless. Their best had simply not been good enough.

"All right," he said. "Paul and I will do it. You try and get some rest."

Rest? How could she rest after such an ordeal. There was a way. The only way. Yesterday, after a day shift, Julie had written a prescription for Amy Smith, and signed it Julie Dalton, M.D. *It is only for emergency,* she told herself. At a drug store, far from the hospital, she'd gone to the pharmacy and looked around while the prescription was being filled. When the pharmacist called, "Amy

Smith," she paid no attention at first.

That's supposed to be me, she reminded herself after a moment and hurried over. She listened patiently as the pharmacist told her of possible side effects. Julie paid for the prescription and slipped the sleeping pills into her purse.

It's not as if I have to have these, she now told herself. But a child had died. Julie had not been able to save that little life. Sure, Dr. Thomas and Luke were more experienced and in charge, but she was part of the team. It was not anyone's fault. They had done everything within their power. But that didn't make it easy. She could still see that lifeless body in her mind. The little girl would never run and play and be a part of her family's life.

With shaking hands, Julie removed the cap from the bottle of pills. She would need two tonight. If ever there was a reason for a sleeping pill, it was now, and she refused to feel guilty about it. Whether for Amy Smith or Julie Dalton, surely this treatment would be highly recommended by any doctor.

❧

There had been no changes in Bobby's condition. Luke knew he was dwelling on that fact too much. He tried to be objective, but that little boy had touched his heartstrings more than he would have imagined. Then another emergency occurred, requiring his total attention.

Late Friday night, Luke fell into an exhausted sleep, then awoke refreshed and spent the entire morning with his boys. The temperature was in the mid-seventies—a perfect day for splashing around in the pool. Trish joined them for almost an hour before going in to prepare a picnic lunch which they enjoyed under the shade of an umbrella over a round table. It was almost like old times.

"I'm so glad you're home, Dad," five-year-old Caleb remarked.

Mark chirped, "Me, too."

"So am I," Luke said, smiling at his boys. Couldn't Trish see that this was quality time—more important than how many times he was home for dinner or whether he tucked them in at night? "But you guys get to play like this every-day, don't you?"

"Rearing children is life's most important job," Trish said. "At least, that's what you said when you wanted me to stay home and start a family." She looked at the boys. "You guys go rinse off and get changed."

"Oh, Mom. . ." Caleb began.

"You know you don't stay out in the hot sun too long," she said. They gave her a disappointed look and sent a helpless glance toward their dad. After they went inside, Trish took up the conversation where it had left off.

"It's not all play, Luke. You see, being with them all the time makes me the disciplinarian, which means I'm the villain and you're the good guy."

"I could have told them to go inside, Trish," he remarked.

"It's not that. It's just that I feel like you think every day is just play and no work."

Hearing the edge in her voice rankled him. "I know it's important to play with your children, Trish. But where's the work in that?"

Trish took a deep breath. "Who do you think will go into the bathroom and pick up wet bathing suits? Clean up the watery mess? Comb their hair? Pick up out here? Straighten up the kitchen?"

"Is that so hard, Trish?"

"No. I love taking care of my family. I just don't feel like you see it as important as. . .as saving lives."

He looked down, shaking his head. "I didn't save a life last night. The child died."

"Oh, Luke, I'm so sorry." Guilt washed over her. Her problems couldn't begin to compare with Luke's. Her everyday life was a breeze compared with the life-and-death situations he faced daily. *It's just that I love him so much,* she was thinking. *I want him to appreciate me.* She was about to tell him so when his next words stopped her cold.

"It was really hard on Julie," he said. "It was her first experience of losing a patient."

Trish blurted out, "She didn't do the surgery, did she?"

"She assisted, Trish. Just as I did when I was a resident. Remember?" His voice sounded as cold as Trish felt. "You used to want details. You empathized with me. That's what I'm doing with Julie. You know she's my responsibility for two more years."

Rankled, Trish retorted sharply, "Well, I happen to be your responsibility for life! So are the children! But do we ever see you? No! And when I do, what do you talk about? Julie!"

She jumped up and began clearing the table.

"Come on, Trish. Don't tell me you're jealous of Julie."

"Should I be?"

Luke snorted but didn't bother to answer. Trish strode toward the house with the tray of paper plates and cups. His eyes followed his wife. Trish was a beautiful woman, no doubt about that. But she'd turned into a nag. And her question kept turning around in his mind.

Should you be jealous of Julie, a good-natured, spirited,

happy young woman who handles life with courage and purpose? Should you be jealous of a woman who can converse on topics that interest me and makes me feel like I'm doing something worthwhile with my life? Trish, you make me feel inadequate. I don't come up to your standards. I'm not a good husband and father. Should you be jealous?

You bet!

Trish and Luke were cordial for the rest of the day. The family went out for pizza and then took in a movie. The boys had a good time, and Luke realized it would protect his sons from hearing their parents argue. Whatever their troubles, he and Trish had the best interests of the boys at heart and wanted to give the appearance of a stable, happy family.

❧

Since Luke had duty on Sunday, he couldn't go to church with them the next day, so Trish invited Marcus home for lunch. She cleaned up while Marcus and the boys played games. Later, while the boys were resting, watching a video, she and Marcus sat in the shade of the patio roof.

As the afternoon progressed, Marcus realized his daughter-in-law was trying to hide a great unhappiness. While he didn't want to push a confidence, he also knew how isolated she could feel. She certainly couldn't confide to the wives of Luke's colleagues about her problems. Maybe he could be of some help.

"Trish," he asked quietly, "what's troubling you?"

"I wish Luke were more like you, Marcus. You're so good with the children, so patient, put them ahead of your own self. You work, but you're never too busy for us. You spend more time with the boys than their own father."

"His work is more demanding, Trish. I have more time. And I need these kids. I don't have a wife, you know, and no one to really share my life with."

Trish bit on her lip to keep back the tears. "Neither does Luke. . .anymore." She shook her head. "He doesn't want me anymore, Marcus. He doesn't love me anymore."

"Now, Trish—" Marcus began.

"No, it's true. People fall out of love. And, he has."

"You want me to talk to him?"

"No," Trish said abruptly. "That would just give him another reason to dislike me. He hates me, Marcus."

"Trish, you know that's not true."

"You know the saying, hate is very close to love. This is love in reverse. We can't talk, we argue. He thinks I don't understand him. Well, I understand him quite well. Too well—and that's his problem. It's not me who's on his mind, Marcus. It's Julie."

"Julie? His assistant?"

"She's all he talks about."

Marcus's mind leaped into the past to that time when his own marriage had been so troubled. He hadn't liked his wife. It was as if the commitment to her had grown null and void. His feelings had been hostile toward her. He'd thought she didn't understand what it took to pass his bar exam or how important it was to him. She'd even said if he didn't pass it the first time, and many didn't, he could take it again, as if failure to pass or waiting to begin his career was of no consequence.

That had infuriated him. He'd thought she didn't care. Only years later did he come to realize she was right. It wouldn't have been the end of the world if he'd had to take it over. It would only have wounded his pride.

But it could have been the end of the world for his children if he and his wife had separated—if he had not remained and been a father to them, if he had not realized that he needed the Lord's help to be the kind of man he should be.

Marcus listened with a sense of familiarity as Trish poured out her doubts. "They seem trivial when I say them, don't they, Marcus? We don't have any big problems like the families affected by the school bus accident. I don't know, maybe it's just me."

"I can't say, Trish. But I know you two were in love when you married. And obviously, you still love Luke."

She nodded. "I just feel like I'm losing him."

"Marriages go through a lot of changes, Trish. People grow and change. It's not easy. Since you don't want me to talk to Luke, I can't speak for him. But let me give you a little advice. Although it may seem unfair and contrary to your natural reactions, don't lash out at him. Make him believe you understand the burden of his work."

"I really do," she admitted.

"Then remind him of your love. When he comes home, don't tell him he doesn't appreciate you. Just share your good experiences of the day. I don't know if a man can ever truly understand the effort it takes to be a good homemaker. I knew a little along the way, but not completely until after Bev died. I now know it takes up a lot of time just in daily living, shopping, cooking, laundry, keeping things straight. And I'm just one person. That's why I hired a housekeeper."

She smiled, and her eyes filled with tears. She laid her hand on his arm. "I wish you could find someone, Marcus."

"I'm all right," he said, but an unusual thought crossed

his mind. He had been satisfied as a widower for years. But suddenly the idea of having a wife seemed appealing, and he didn't really want to admit why.

eleven

Marcus wondered how he could approach Sharon—or if he should. This was such a difficult time in her life, trying to cope with her losses. She wouldn't be thinking of any kind of relationship with a man—not with every moment spent concentrating on her grandson's recovery.

It wasn't the kind of situation where he could just invite her out to dinner. No doubt, she wouldn't go any farther than the hospital cafeteria. He couldn't think of any way he might be of assistance to her, other than through what he'd already done. But that had been minor. The legal papers he'd looked over had been easy. Her mother left her everything—period!

Maybe he should remember what he'd said to Trish. He didn't have a woman in his life, and that meant he had time for his grandchildren. He'd been content with that for several years, even though he had enjoyed an occasional companionable dinner with a woman. He shouldn't be thinking of anything more serious.

But he was. Even when he responded to the buzzer indicating he had a call on line two.

"Marcus?"

"Speaking."

"This is Sharon Martin. I don't want to impose but you did say to call if I needed—"

"I meant it," he interrupted, elation being replaced by concern. "Is Bobby all right?"

"Oh, he's improving by leaps and bounds," she said. "But I need some legal advice."

"Do you want me to come to the hospital?"

"When it's convenient."

Marcus pushed aside the file folders on his desk. "What about lunch?" He added quickly, "In the hospital cafeteria."

❧

After her initial shock wore off, Sharon could not feel anger at Mary and James for wanting custody of Bobby. She knew they loved him. He was their deceased daughter's child—their first and only grandchild—but her home in California was the only home Bobby had ever known.

Sharon wanted what was best for Bobby. But how could she stand it if the best wasn't herself? She knew she had to put aside her resolve not to be involved with Marcus and instead follow through on his offer to give legal advice. Marcus had seemed eager to meet her. She was glad he suggested the cafeteria. She didn't want to be away from Bobby for too long now that Mary and James had returned to California.

Her heart skipped a beat, seeing that Marcus was waiting for her at a small table near a window. She chose a salad and skim milk, then sat opposite him.

"Shall we say grace?" he asked.

Sharon could have cried listening to Marcus's words while he offered a prayer of thanks and asked for wisdom to deal with life's difficulties. How different from her encounter with him twenty-three years ago. This is how a relationship should develop. But that was not possible in this instance.

After the prayer, before taking a bite of his veggie-burger, he asked, "How can I help you, Sharon?"

She told him about Mary and James wanting custody of Bobby. "I don't want Bobby to feel the tension of his grandparents fighting a battle in court," Sharon said. "But what choice do I have?"

"Tell me about Mary and James," Marcus urged.

Sharon told about their characters, their son and daughter, their lifestyle, their past involvement with Bobby. She feared this conflict would permanently damage her relationship with Mary and James. How could it ever be reconciled?

"Surely," she added after giving him the information, "a judge would take into account that I have been the mother figure for Bobby."

"We know that was your role, Sharon," Marcus said. "But a judge might see it differently. Many children are taken to baby-sitters or day-care workers until their parents get off work, but a judge wouldn't give custody to those persons."

"If Bobby could choose, he would choose me. He and his parents lived in my home in California. I was with him every moment."

"Yes, and if I were the judge, I'd choose you, but a judge has to try to be impartial and act according to the law. There is no doubt you have been like a mother to Bobby. However, the maternal grandparents, being of high moral character as you indicate and with two teenagers in the home, have an edge. It's a family, Sharon, with a male authority figure in the home.

"My suggestion is to continue as you have in the past. Give Bobby the best of care, and stay on good terms with Mary and James. They may think differently after some time has passed. Right now, they're trying to hold onto a part of their daughter."

Sharon closed her eyes for a moment. "How could I manage without him?"

"You have him right now," Marcus said. "Just take it a day at a time."

Her warm gaze met his eyes. A slight turn of her lips indicated she would try that. "I know you're right. God has a way of bringing so much good from a situation that looks hopeless."

He smiled, nodding, knowing what she meant.

❧

For the next few weeks, Sharon did as Marcus suggested and as she had done many times in the past: she took things one day at a time. The IVs were removed from Bobby's arms, but he still had to be medicated for pain and to keep him from becoming so active that he'd risk damage to his internal organs while they healed. He had settled into a routine of long morning and afternoon naps as well as sleeping through the night.

He called for his mommy and daddy a time or two, but seemed content when Sharon told him they couldn't come right now and she would tell him all about it later. She had been with Bobby almost every moment of his life. His parents had worked days, had even taken vacations without him. But Sharon had always been there for him, making sure he felt loved and secure.

There had not been a need for additional surgery. It was still uncertain what damage the head trauma might have done, but the swelling on the brain was receding, and Bobby was slowly coming out of his coma. His eyes had began to flutter open, would alight on Sharon, then close. She continued to spend nights in his room and spend most of her time during the day there as well so he would feel secure whenever he opened his eyes.

On Monday morning after the nurse had bathed him and he'd seemed to be breathing deeply as he slept, Sharon was answering mail that continued to come in with encouraging words. She looked over at his face. Something looked different. His face seemed more peaceful. Then she saw his eyelids quiver.

"Bobby?" Sharon whispered, hurrying over to the chair next to the bed, where she often sat and stroked his arm and talked or prayed aloud. She touched his forehead.

His eyes slowly opened but appeared glazed, and he didn't seem to recognize her before they closed again. Was there brain damage? She pressed a button, and a nurse's voice over the intercom immediately asked, "Do you need something?"

"I think Bobby's waking up," Sharon said in a soft, hopeful voice.

"I'll send someone in," the nurse said.

Sharon kept talking, telling Bobby she was with him, touching his face, his arm, his hand. His lips moved, but no sound came. Oh, how she wanted to see his eyes open, to hear his voice, to know he would be whole and healthy again. "So many people love you, darling. Can you please wake up?"

His eyes moved beneath his lids, and they slowly opened again. This time his gaze held hers a little longer, in spite of the drowsy look.

By that time, the nurse came in. She was taking his temperature when Julie appeared and began to listen to his heart. Luke wasn't far behind. "The monitors indicate the swelling has almost completely receded," Luke said. "He probably is coming out of his coma." He watched as

Julie checked Bobby's eyes.

Bobby tried to move away from the light. Julie stepped back and looked at Luke, then Sharon, with a huge smile on her face. She nodded.

Luke was obviously delighted that Bobby was regaining consciousness. "He's a little fighter."

"Yes, yes he is," Sharon agreed. "Bobby, this is Grandmother, honey."

His head turned toward her. His eyes focused for a short time, but long enough that Sharon knew he recognized her. A sound came from his throat. Luke said that was good. He was trying to talk, but it might take awhile.

Sharon would not leave the room now for anything. Her lunch was brought in to her. It was afternoon when it happened again. This time Bobby's eyes looked tired, but he muttered, "Granmudder." Then she watched as his eyes tried to focus as they looked around the room. They lit upon the dinosaur.

"Di-sor," he said in a tiny, weak voice.

"Yes, darling," Sharon said and put the stuffed animal next to him so his cheek could brush against its plush fur. He tried to move his arms, but they were fastened down so he wouldn't be able to thrash around or pull out the IVs.

Sharon explained that he'd been hurt in an accident but was going to be fine. He drifted away again, and an hour later he awoke. "Granmudder," he said.

Sharon asked if he remembered that she told him he had been in an accident and was in the hospital, and he said yes. She thought that was a sign that his little mind was working just fine. "Mommy," he said.

"I'll tell you about Mommy and Daddy later, darling. Right now, just rest and get well, so I can take you home."

She told him about his grandparents having come to visit.

During visiting hours, Marcus came. He brought one of Caleb and Mark's videos and a monkey holding a plastic balloon that read "Get well soon."

"Luke told me the wonderful news," he said excitedly, coming into the room, then went right over to Bobby, whose eyes were closed. Marcus told him what he'd brought. Bobby opened his eyes and stared at Marcus. His little eyes lit up when he looked at the monkey, and his lips tried to smile.

Sharon felt her heart would burst. This was the first look that had passed between Bobby and his grandfather. Neither knew. Would they ever?

twelve

Sharon thought that when Dickens wrote, "It was the best of times, it was the worst of times," he must have had her situation in mind. It was that way with Bobby and with Marcus.

She couldn't be happier that Bobby's complete recovery appeared imminent. She hired a private nurse for when Bobby would leave the hospital. The nurse, a very competent young woman named Lisa, was recommended by Luke. She was a good nurse but didn't want to work full-time and had been looking for the kind of private duty that suited her. She worked on the pediatric floor and had already fallen in love with Bobby, as had the entire city so it seemed.

Lisa gave the hospital notice that she would leave the hospital at the end of the month and began to come into Bobby's room whenever she could. Finally she was assigned to duty as his day nurse.

Along with the expectations of taking Bobby home in a few weeks, Sharon felt a terrible dread as the time grew closer when his maternal grandparents would seek custody. She couldn't possibly let that child go without a fight. At the same time, she wondered if she had enough courage to enter into a court battle against people she'd come to love and respect. However, she would do what she thought best for Bobby.

A couple of days after Bobby awoke, he'd asked for his

mommy. Sharon had waited until he asked, then explained there had been a car wreck. His mommy and daddy were now in heaven with Jesus.

"Want Mommy 'n' Daddy," he protested.

"I know, darling. So do I. But they are with Jesus in heaven. He wanted you to stay here with me and others who love you so much, like Grandma Mary, Grandpa James, Aunt Kim, Uncle Brad."

"And dem," he said. Sharon looked around to see that Luke and Julie were coming into the room. He must instinctively know how these doctors had cared about him, gently examined and talked to him.

"What's this all about?" Luke asked playfully.

Bobby giggled.

"We were talking about all the people who love him," Sharon said, moving back so the doctors could examine Bobby.

"I'd better be on that list," Luke said as Bobby looked trustingly at Luke, not just his doctor, but his uncle.

Sharon looked out the window for a long moment, thinking that Mitchell died before Bobby was born. None of Mitchell's relatives had even visited after he died.

How wonderful if Bobby could know his daddy's relatives—Uncle Luke in this room and others not very far away: Grandfather Marcus, Aunt Trish, Aunt Kathleen, Uncle Brian, Cousin Caleb, and Cousin Mark. These were his paternal relatives. Must he never know?

"One day at a time," Marcus had said.

Yes, she thought, *I will not worry but do whatever I think is best for my only relative in the world—my precious Bobby*.

She could capture picture memories for Bobby on film.

She could get a video camera and film Luke with Bobby. She could tape Marcus stopping in to visit, bringing books and videos, as he had insisted his grandsons wanted him to do. She would keep the tape, along with the newspaper clippings she had in California about Marcus and his family. Someday, when Bobby grew up, he would want to know about his background. She could give him more than a verbal description. He could be proud of his dad's relatives.

When Marcus called to say that he wouldn't be able to get away from court to visit Bobby that day and asked if he could do anything, Sharon told him about wanting to get a video camera.

Marcus had a better idea. She could use his. It was rarely used anymore. Luke had his own that was used for family gatherings and capturing events involving Caleb and Mark.

He brought it the next day and took turns filming Bobby with his grandmother, with Lisa, and with the children in the playroom where Bobby was allowed to watch for the first time.

Later, when Luke and Julie came in to check on Bobby, Luke gave his dad and the video camera a mock annoyed look. "I guess you know, Dad, I wouldn't allow just anybody to do that."

Marcus laughed. "That's an advantage of being a father," he said.

"But in this hospital, the doctor's word is law, not the judge's," Luke retorted.

Julie and Sharon laughed, and so did Bobby, although Sharon didn't think he understood the light bantering. But he could understand the feeling of camaraderie that passed between Marcus and Luke. She was glad the conversation, too, was captured for Bobby to hear at some later time.

Oddly, it was the video camera that seemed to break down any barriers between her and Marcus. It was always there to turn to, to use, to focus attention upon. Bobby was becoming a regular little actor, saving his best performances for Marcus and the camera. Bobby was excited when Sharon told him she would fix up her mother's bedroom for him and would find some wallpaper to make it just right for when he'd go home in a few weeks.

Sharon rather regretted when Marcus asked, "What kind of pictures do you want on your wallpaper?" She knew it could be some impossible request, but hoped it might be "Di-sor."

"Booey Beese," he said.

"What's that again?" Marcus questioned, glancing at Sharon, who grinned.

"Dis!" His finger stabbed the book that Mark had said he'd like—*Beauty and the Beast*.

"Oh, I think we can handle that," Marcus said confidently.

"Can we?" Sharon wasn't so sure. Especially about the "we" part.

However, when Lisa came in after Bobby's supper to sit and read to him, Marcus insisted that Sharon allow him to help her find "Booey-Beese" wallpaper.

❧

Marcus could hardly believe how much he'd changed in the short time he'd known Sharon. Driving her to a home-decorating store and looking for *Beauty and the Beast* wallpaper had suddenly become the most important moment of his day. During the past few years he'd enjoyed going out to dinner or a special function with a woman but was always glad to be going home alone, to his comfortable home where he liked his own space, his own peace and quiet. Lately, however, that peace and quiet had turned to loneliness. And he'd found himself thinking how nice it would be to share that home with someone, and invariably Sharon was on his mind.

"You don't need to go in, Marcus," Sharon said. "I know a lot of men hate to shop."

He'd never particularly liked it. But he wanted to do this. His smile was broad. "I'm looking forward to this," he said.

As it turned out, that pattern was popular in a couple of designs, and they decided to accentuate the cartoon-characters and downplay the Beast without overdoing the Beauty. After getting the wallpaper, Marcus delighted in Sharon's appreciation of his reminding her they'd need paste, brushes, a cutter, and other tools.

"I thought you just wet it and hung it," she said.

Marcus laughed. "Have you never hung wallpaper before?"

"Like I mentioned before," she said, as if redeeming herself for not being an expert wallpaper hanger, "Mitchell was a builder. Our house is very modern, mainly white, and no wallpaper."

At last, he thought on the way to her house, *I've found a way to spend time with her. And whether or not she knows it, she will need me with this project.*

After unloading the materials in the kitchen, they went into her mother's bedroom that was to be remodeled for Bobby. Marcus sighed and shook his head, pretending chagrin. "I may be taking my life in my hands, but I'm willing to help you."

"Taking your life in your hands?" she questioned.

"Hanging wallpaper together leads to violence," he said, "as does teaching someone to drive a car."

Sharon laughed. "Oh, I've heard things like that, but I suspect it's grossly exaggerated. My dad taught me to drive when I was fifteen. We had no problems. Really, I think we can handle it. After all, we're both adults."

His glance was skeptical, but he said, "First thing is to get this furniture out of here."

"Really, Marcus. I can hire someone to do this."

He gazed at her thoughtfully, then grinned, "Let's try it together. I haven't had a good fight in a long time."

&

Sharon had liked Marcus's playfulness about their possibly fighting while hanging wallpaper, but she certainly had no intention of their project coming close to blows. She appreciated his willingness to help. Two nights later, however, after her mother's furniture had been stored away in the basement and they'd begun to cut, measure, paste, and hang, she did find a few things slightly irritating.

"You've got to let go if I'm going to match this up," Marcus said, standing on the ladder.

"You just told me to push the seams together and hold them."

"Right, after I get things lined up at the top."

"You didn't say that, Marcus."

"I expected you to know."

"Are you calling me stupid?" she asked and pulled the paper away from the wall.

"Now you've torn it," he said, letting go. The entire sheet tumbled down.

"Me? I'm not the one pulling and tugging and telling

me to line up the seams, then saying let go. You have the easy part."

He came down. "Okay, we'll cut another piece, and you get up there."

She felt like lashing out at him, or crying, or something, but refused to let him see she was upset. He was helping. But she should have hired it done. Her hands trembled as she tried to cut along the metal square. Her eyes became blurry.

"Here, let me," Marcus said gently. "I'm sorry."

She sniffed. "So am I."

He cut the paper. She helped him turn it over on the kitchen table, and they were very careful to fold at the right places as he brushed on the paste.

He carried the folded piece into the bedroom, and Sharon climbed the ladder. She caught hold of the edges and matched it at the top, feeling she had redeemed herself. However, as he began to unfold the piece, her fingers relaxed. The weight of the paper pulled it off the wall and right down on his head.

"Get this stuff off me!" he yelled.

Sharon gasped, then began to laugh. "Don't move. You just hold it right there." Marcus stood stiff as a board while she hurried to get the video camera. "Oh, this is great," she said, still laughing while the camera began to grind.

"I'm sorry, Marcus," she said, "But this is priceless."

After filming for awhile from various angles, she put the camera down and went over to pick the wallpaper off him. "I shouldn't have done that, should I?"

He acted gruff. "People have gotten divorced over things like this."

She stared into his eyes, and they began to dance. "Of course," he added, "they have to get married first."

Sharon stopped her laughing and would not look into his eyes again. "Your hair is full of paste. Let's go back to the way we started."

Her eyes met his again, and she knew he thought what she did. They should go back, not just to his climbing the ladder, but to subjects that did not get too personal.

He climbed the ladder, and they continued with precision, each more careful than before.

"It's beautiful," Sharon exclaimed when they'd finished with the long pieces, and cleaned up the mess.

Marcus nodded. "Looks pretty good," he said. "Even though you did throw wet wallpaper at me."

Sharon laughed. "You'd better get that paste out of your hair. There's shampoo in the bathroom."

While Marcus was shampooing his hair, Sharon called Mary and James, having figured that with the time difference the couple should be home from work and have finished supper. She wanted to keep them informed about Bobby's progress.

They were delighted that Bobby might soon be going home.

"I hope you're taking some time for yourself, Sharon," Mary said.

"Yes, I leave the hospital occasionally, usually after supper when Lisa comes in and reads to him. He goes to sleep right after that and doesn't awaken until morning."

"You go out alone?"

"Not always. You remember Marcus?"

"The judge?" James put in from another phone.

"Yes, he has been very helpful with things like legal matters." She also told them about his helping with the wallpaper.

"It would be wonderful if you had a man in your life, Sharon," Mary said.

"Oh, no. It's not like that. I'll be returning to California as soon as Bobby is well. We'll talk then, Mary, James."

"Are you angry with us, Sharon?" Mary asked gently.

Sharon took a deep breath. "Not angry. Oh, Mary, you and James please pray about this. I want what is best for Bobby. I. . .we'll talk about it when I return. Okay?"

"Sharon, we're not trying to hurt you, and this is not against you."

"Yes, I know, Mary. Like me, you want what is best for Bobby."

She stared at the phone for a long moment after they said their good-byes.

What would a judge think was best for Bobby?

Just then, she heard Marcus coming out of the bathroom. When she turned and saw him, towel-drying his hair, she smiled. "Would you like a sandwich?"

While they ate in the kitchen, Marcus said they could paste the border on the following day.

"I don't know if that's a good idea," she replied, and laughed. "After today's fiasco."

He smiled. "Haven't you heard? A couple who survives wallpapering together can handle anything."

"Oh?" she quipped. "I thought the saying was about praying together."

The smile left his lips, and he looked across at her seriously. "We've done that too."

Sharon swallowed a bite too large and quickly took a sip of tea. Her heart leaped at the implication. But at the same time, she knew there could never be a close relationship between her and Marcus, because to tell him the truth would destroy their relationship.

"I will have to return to California as soon as Bobby is well enough," she reminded him.

"Would you consider returning to Mount Pleasant? If not permanently, then visits throughout the year. Where there's a will, there's a way, you know."

Oh, if things were different. If there were not that one night of indiscretion twenty-three years ago, she would be willing to discuss that, and pursue a serious relationship with this wonderful man. Although the past could be forgiven, it could not be erased.

She shook her head. "I believe Bobby needs me, Marcus. If I don't get custody, I will still have to be nearby. Although he loves Mary and James, I know he would be devastated without me. If I do get custody, how could I take him from Mary and James?"

"It is a dilemma," Marcus admitted. "In the meantime, Sharon, I want to say that my time spent with you means a lot to me. I hope it can continue as long as you are here."

Sharon looked away. She couldn't see how there might be a future together for the two of them. But if the most there could be were memories, she would treasure them forever.

thirteen

Intent on helping Sharon get her mother's house ready for Bobby's release from the hospital, Marcus talked to Luke and Trish about their baby furniture. Both were eager to allow Sharon to borrow a youth bed that was stored in their basement. There was also a high chair that might be useful in helping confine Bobby instead of letting him run around too much before his body was ready.

When the day came to pick up the furniture, for a moment Sharon felt like she couldn't possibly go to the house where Marcus and Bev had lived, where they had reared their children. Then she told herself that was exactly what she should do to keep her own resolve in perspective. She must face reality and entertain no thoughts about a serious relationship between her and Marcus.

Sharon was soon put at ease by Trish's obvious delight in meeting her. Luke came home early for a change. He and Trish insisted Sharon and Marcus have dinner with them. Trish had beef roast, potatoes, onions, and carrots smothered in cream of mushroom soup warming in the oven, ready for the table.

Sharon's resistance to their dinner invitation didn't last long with Luke, Trish, and Marcus laying out the reasons why this was more practical and would get her back to the hospital more quickly than if she went home and prepared something for herself.

After dinner, they all settled on the patio with cool

lemonade while the boys rode their bikes on the concrete around the pool. Sharon spoke of it reminding her of her own home in California.

When Sharon mentioned that she would return to California when Bobby was well, she didn't notice the darkening of Marcus's face. Trish did, however, and after the older couple left, she mentioned to Luke how it might be nice for his father to have a woman like Sharon in his life permanently. For the first time in a long time, they actually agreed on something. Luke even agreed that Trish and the boys might take a birthday gift to Bobby. He had told Sharon she could have a small gathering and even a cake. A big party or too much excitement wouldn't be good for him at this time, but Bobby had come to rely on Luke to care for him and upon Marcus to visit with him almost every day.

"I think it would be a nice gesture," Luke said to Trish, "if you and the boys were there as well."

Remembering Marcus's advice, Trish bit her tongue to keep from asking if Julie would be there. Of course she would. She was the resident physician, Luke's trainee. That's what Luke would have said had she asked.

⁂

It started out as a lovely day. At two in the afternoon, Trish, Caleb, and Mark arrived for the party. Marcus, Sharon, and Lisa were already in the room. A cake with blue frosting, a small car, and three candles sat on the portable eating tray. On the dresser were clown-decorated paper plates, napkins, cups, and apple juice.

Sharon was videotaping all the happenings.

Bobby got to sit in a chair for this occasion. As soon as Luke came in, they all sang "Happy Birthday" to Bobby.

Almost immediately, Luke left because he had to see other patients.

Marcus took the camera while Sharon lit the candles and rolled the table over to Bobby.

"Make a wish," Caleb said.

"I wish—I wish—"

"No, it won't come true if you say it out loud," Caleb warned. "Make a wish and blow out the candles."

Bobby blew, and all three candles were out on the second try. Sharon noticed how much weaker his breaths had been than before the accident. She was thankful her grandson was healing, but obviously he was still very weak.

Bobby appeared stronger, however, when he tore into the presents. Luke and Trish gave him a doctor's kit.

"I got one like that," Mark told him.

Marcus got him a picture book that made sounds when he pressed certain buttons. "You're gonna like this," Mark said when Bobby began to open his present. It was a black dragon with orange wings that could be clipped off and on and flapped up and down.

Caleb gave him a video of the popular children's series of *Cupcakes,* acting out Christian principles. "That one's adorable," Trish said. "It's based on a true story of a child who fell off a cliff in North Carolina and was saved by the creator of these videos. He used his cupcake voices to keep her calm until rescuers could get to her."

"I haven't heard of these," Sharon said.

"They haven't been on the market very long," Trish explained.

"I can vouch for them, too," Marcus said. "They're great baby-sitters and teachers at the same time."

"Oh, so that's what you guys do at your house, Marcus?" Trish quipped.

"At least one hour out of the entire day." He laughed. "Those grandsons of mine wouldn't sit still longer than that."

Lisa brought him a book of Bible stories. There was a gift from Julie—a bank in the shape of a clown that reached out to grab the coins and put them in the top of his head.

Sharon got Bobby a small farm with animals that might keep him occupied. It wouldn't be easy to keep a three-year-old boy down once he felt better, and he was showing every sign of that.

"Oh, neat," Caleb said. "I like that horse."

"Maybe you and Mark can come and play with Bobby sometime," Sharon said. She was operating the camera again.

"I wished I could play now," Bobby said, starting to get down from the chair.

"Hold it, buddy," said a voice from the doorway. Luke had returned. "You have to rest now, so you'll feel like playing later."

"Can I eat some cake?"

"One piece, then to bed for a nap. Your toys will be waiting for you."

❧

Trish knew she should have known better than to broach the subject of Julie again. And yet, the past few days' camaraderie with Luke had given her a false sense of security, as if things were back to the way they used to be. So that evening she brought the subject up.

"I thought Julie would be at Bobby's party."

"She had the day off," Luke said shortly.

Trish felt dismayed that Luke acted defensively if she even said Julie's name. "Right, but Bobby was your top priority for so long, I still thought she would have at least dropped by. I mean, you talked about how concerned she was about him, how much you two had to consult on his condition."

Seeing the cloud cover Luke's face, Trish knew she was treading in deep water. But she should be able to mention Julie without it becoming some kind of issue.

"She needed time away from her work, Trish. She asked me to take Bobby's present to him."

"It just seemed strange, that's all."

"No, Trish. The unusual part is that doctors get presents for patients in the first place."

"Not a patient like Bobby," Trish contradicted. "He has attracted the attention of the entire city, if not the nation."

"Then you might ask Julie why she wasn't at the party, if it's that important to you, Trish. She will be among our guests for the cookout."

Last year, the annual early summer cookout was at Paul Thomas's home. This year, it was Luke's turn. And Julie would be here. Trish dreaded seeing the woman she'd like to sue for alienation of her husband's affection. Maybe it would prove the opposite, however—that her fears were based on an overactive imagination. Maybe she was unnecessarily jealous because Julie had a closeness with Luke in a way she did not.

Trish knew how closely residents and physicians worked together, how much they collaborated and depended upon each other, and how each valued the other's expertise. She also knew that Luke considered Julie the brightest, prettiest, most valuable resident he'd ever trained.

"Are you up to it, Trish?" Luke asked, bringing her back to the issue at hand.

"I'm looking forward to it, Luke," she said, and knew that pleased him. It was important to him to entertain his colleagues. And he needed a little relaxation. She was determined to make a good impression on Luke and their friends and was determined to stop imagining things that were probably only in her own mind. Luke was her husband. He came home to her every night, even if it was usually late and even if his conversation centered on Julie more than on her.

Actually, Trish hadn't realized that the cookout would be upon them in little over a week. Her days were fuller than usual, now that Caleb was out of school. She would ask Kathleen to keep the boys overnight. Marcus would be happy to help, but she wanted him at the cookout. He knew all the doctors anyway and was friends with a couple of them.

To be honest, she wanted Marcus there. He gave her confidence, but she also wanted his opinion about Luke and Julie after seeing them together in this informal setting. Maybe he would convince her that her imagination had run away with her or that any suspicions were totally unfounded. No, Trish decided, she'd ask for her mom's help and would borrow Marcus's housekeeper.

If she did it well enough, maybe she and Luke could have a romantic evening afterward. Guests would be arriving around four to take advantage of the pool, lounge on the patio, and play games in the basement rec room. Generally at these gathering, they ate around six, and guests began to leave by eight o'clock. Trish and Luke had always left as soon as politely able, eager to return home and spend the evening together—that is, before they began to drift apart after she became so busy with the children.

Maybe if she worked it right, Luke would appreciate her efforts and maybe see her, not just as his wife and the mother of his children, but as an attractive, appealing woman. They'd have the entire night alone, and the boys wouldn't come home the next day until she called Kathleen. Yes, maybe this would be the perfect time for she and Luke to get back on track.

And maybe Julie would make an excuse not to come.

That thought frightened Trish. She wanted Luke to tell her that his feelings for Julie were strictly on a business level. She wanted Julie to bring a boyfriend. The last thing she wanted was confirmation that her suspicions were true. Before now, she had not allowed herself to think what could happen to her marriage, to her family.

While continuing to make plans, Trish began to dread the reality of what she might discover at the cookout.

*

Marcus looked forward to the cookout and asked Sharon to join him. She gave several excuses why she shouldn't. She didn't want to infringe on his family's gatherings. She didn't want to leave Bobby for very long. Then she laughed and asked if he were so desperate for a date.

He smiled. "No, I've dated several women. And my friends manage to let me know they've invited a spare woman at couples' parties. This one doesn't require a date. But I'm asking you, Sharon."

She didn't consent until after Luke invited her. After examining Bobby, he had given her the good news. Bobby could go home on Sunday.

"Oh, Luke, thank you. Thank you so much." She couldn't resist hugging him. Feeling his strong young arms around her, for a moment she reveled in the thought that this was her son's half brother. Grief and joy threatened to overwhelm her. She stepped back and wiped her eyes with a tissue.

He smiled warmly. "Now, you are to take some time out for yourself," he said. "Doctor's orders. And on the agenda is a cookout at my house next Saturday."

"Oh, I wouldn't know anyone," she said.

"You know me. Trish. Caleb. Mark. Marcus. Julie. Paul Thomas. And you've met several others who'll be there. Also, my sister, Kathleen, and her husband, Bo, want to meet you."

Bobby had received a card from Kathleen and Bo, wishing him a speedy recovery. Sharon reminded herself that the past was past and there was no real reason why she should refuse. Besides, she wanted to meet this daughter of Marcus's. She could file that memory along with others to tell Bobby about someday. Until now, she'd almost forgotten how she'd enjoyed such gatherings when Mitchell was alive.

Trish calling to invite Sharon clinched her decision. And it wasn't as if she or Marcus thought there was anything between them other than friendship. Now with Bobby's release scheduled to take place in a couple of days, the time was drawing closer when she would return to California.

When Marcus called that afternoon, Sharon told him she couldn't be away from Bobby for an entire afternoon and evening but would drop in for awhile if all was well with Bobby.

"Trish told me you accepted," Marcus said. "How did

she manage to convince you?"

"She agreed to let me bring a batch of cookies from my mother's secret recipe."

"I'll let you bring cookies this evening if you'll have dinner with me, at my house."

"I haven't made the cookies yet, so I'll bring a special one for you to the cookout. But seriously, Marcus, I do want to talk to you about something."

"That's what I was about to say to you," he replied. "I'll pick you up at seven."

fourteen

Later that evening, Marcus picked Sharon up in his town car. She liked riding through the streets of historic Charleston. She'd taken this area for granted when she was a young girl and had preferred the more modern neighborhoods.

"Although I lived here when I was young," she said, "I never saw the inside of any historic homes until a few years ago when Mitchell came with me in the spring and we took the historic tour."

"My home is in the historic district, though not on the tour list," Marcus said. "But there's something exciting about seeing crowds of people throng the sidewalks and appreciate the beauty and history of these homes."

He mentioned several they passed, such as the Calhoun Mansion. "If anyone had told me when I was young, that I'd return to the house I grew up in, I would have thought they'd lost their minds." He laughed. "I guess one appreciates history and memories more as one grows older."

"Oh, I think you're definitely right," Sharon said as Marcus pulled into a narrow driveway between two houses very close together as these historic homes typically were built. She liked the smell of the sea and the looks of the cobblestone streets, the decorative wrought-iron railings that bordered the sidewalks and the various designs of homes—Federal, Georgian, Early Victorian. "I particularly like the gardens."

"Be my guest," he said, gesturing straight ahead toward the high iron gate. They got out of the car, and he held open the gate for her to pass through, then fastened it. "It's more colorful when the azaleas are in bloom."

"Oh, but this is lovely," she said, always amazed at how much these Charlestonians could pack into a garden. High wooden walls blocked out any sight of the nearby neighbors, giving complete privacy to the benches and tables surrounded by tall and short bushes, trimmed boxwood, beautiful pink, red, and white anemones, and myriads of plants, now lushly green.

"I admit I don't spend much time gardening," he said.

Sharon noticed, but the possibilities of the space abounded. With a little pruning here, a little weeding there. . . "I like it," she said.

"Since we're right at the back door, do you mind going in this way?"

"I've heard back doors mean the epitome of acceptance," she said and ascended the steps to the back door.

Marcus explained that he'd had some renovations done, such as modernizing the kitchen, while some of the other rooms had been restored to their eighteenth-century designs. "I've even kept some of my parents' furniture, now antiques."

Sharon was anxious to see this two-story, typically narrow home that exhibited so much character. But first she paused for introductions to a short, stout woman who was turning away from the kitchen sink. The woman wiped her hands on a dish towel and smiled at them while Marcus made the introductions.

Her name was Melba, and she said dinner was ready anytime. "You can go right on in to the dining room."

"I'll show you the house later," Marcus said, after he led Sharon into the long, narrow, paneled dining room, dominated by a long table that could seat at least ten people. On it were two place settings of fine china, opposite each other at one end. A crystal chandelier hung from the ceiling.

Old photographs Sharon assumed were of ancestors hung in antique frames on three walls. One wall was dominated by glass windows. The fading light indicated that dusk wasn't far behind. Marcus flipped on the chandelier, giving a cozy glow to the polished mahogany table and the centerpiece of fruit in a silver bowl. Everything was beautiful, but Sharon noted that a woman's touch could brighten and enhance such a lovely home.

She forced that thought away as Marcus held out a chair for her. Sharon hesitated. "Marcus, this is lovely. But I wouldn't mind being less formal."

"Frankly," he admitted, "I never eat here unless there's company. Even Luke and Trish and the boys prefer the kitchen or the serving bar."

"I'd like that," she said and, following his suggestion, moved the place setting to the serving counter that separated the dining area from another room, while Marcus switched on other lights.

"My den," he said, gesturing toward the cozy room that had a definite masculine look to it, with its paneled walls, oversized couch, heavy coffee table, and end tables. A desk was along one wall, flanked by bookshelves from floor to ceiling. A deep-green recliner faced a TV that dominated one corner.

When Melba rolled in a cart from the kitchen, Marcus told her that he and Sharon would eat at the counter. Melba set out gourmet salads with a choice of dressings.

She uncovered a steaming seafood platter and placed before them hot buttered crusty bread. The aroma was fantastic, the food looked better than what any restaurant could serve, and Sharon could hardly wait for Marcus to finish saying grace so she could dig into it.

Melba joined in the "Amen" when Marcus finished saying grace, then gave them iced tea. Sharon felt the woman was waiting to see if everything was all right.

"This is delicious," Sharon said, even before swallowing the bite of tasty catfish, and looking longingly at the crab. "Mmmm, I've never tasted better."

"I agree, Melba. It's perfect."

Melba smiled broadly. "You need anything, just let me know."

Marcus and Sharon talked about the house as they ate. It was after the banana pudding that they settled on the couch in the den, with coffee. Sharon nestled in a corner against several cushions, while Marcus sat near the other end. He set his cup on the coffee table.

The subdued colors of the room and the faint lighting seemed conducive to conversation. She could imagine Marcus sitting at the desk, poring over case studies, or napping on the couch, or reclining in the chair. This room seemed to invite intimacy and warm camaraderie.

"Now," she said, "what did you want to talk to me about?" She sipped her coffee and looked over the rim of the cup at him. Maybe this was a little too intimate, she decided, seeing the warmth in his eyes. Then his expression changed, as if he were reluctant to speak.

"Ladies first," he said and moved farther back on the couch.

"I called Mary and James today and told them about

Bobby's being released from the hospital this coming Sunday."

Marcus nodded for her to continue.

She leaned forward to set her cup down on the table. "I had thought they might change their mind about custody. I told them I would stay in California, but they're more determined than ever. Mary is even willing to quit her job. Her teenagers are excited about the prospect of Bobby coming to live with them. How can I face my home with all my family gone? With Bobby gone?"

"Mary and James don't consider your feelings?"

"Yes, yes they do. But they think this is best for Bobby. And. . .maybe they're right. He would miss me terribly. I've been his stability, the one always there for him. But he's young. He would adjust. But he's like my own child, Marcus. Am I being selfish?"

"Sharon," he said, "I don't think you're being selfish. Your having been his primary caregiver since his birth would hold a lot of weight in court."

Sharon felt a stronger ray of hope. "A judge wouldn't think I'm too old to raise this child?"

"Mary and James are around your age, so that would not be a consideration."

"I have no financial problems, Marcus. The house in California is paid for. Mother's house also. Mitchell's insurance—"

Marcus halted her words with an uplifted hand. "But could Mary and James provide a comfortable living for Bobby?"

"Yes," Sharon admitted.

"Then the financial status would be no consideration." He took a deep breath as if deciding to plunge in. "As I see it, Sharon, you have the advantage of having been Bobby's primary caregiver and having been with him during his recuperation. However, Mary and James have an advantage. They are a married couple. Your chances are good, but they would be better if you were married or planning to be married."

Sharon was shocked into silence. Their eyes held for a long moment, then Sharon swallowed hard and leaned forward to set her cup on the coffee table, lest she drop it. Surely she was misinterpreting. She tried to jest. "I have no such plans. Since Mitchell, there's been no one."

"Sharon, I've known all along that I could fall in love with you. That feeling grows stronger day by day. With all you've been through and your concern for Bobby, I wouldn't expect that you've thought seriously about marriage to anyone. But the matter of custody isn't far off. Do you think you could find it in your heart to consider marriage with me?"

"Marcus, I could not treat you so unfairly by marrying you to get custody of Bobby."

"If you could love me enough, Sharon, for us to build a life together, and if you feel I could be the right father figure for Bobby, then it would be the right thing to do. But even if you say yes, that doesn't guarantee that you would get custody. It could improve your chances."

When she got up from the couch and walked over to the window and stared out into the darkness, Marcus came up beside her.

"I'm sorry, Sharon," he said, "if it's too soon for me to mention this."

No, her mind screamed. *It's too late—twenty-three years too late!*

"There's no problem with loving you, Marcus," Sharon said. She had begun to love him that night on the beach, had loved him in her son, her grandson. Now, she was more strongly drawn to him and found her need for him was even greater in her maturity than in her youth. However, she knew she had to withdraw. It would be disastrous to let him know she bore his child. She wanted and needed his presence with her—he was the father of her only son, grandfather of Bobby. But she could not consider marriage to him without telling him the truth. She could not tell him the truth without bringing up the past, and she knew that would only lead to complete alienation from him.

"Then?" he questioned as he placed his hands on her shoulders and turned her to face him.

She tried to speak, but no words came. Moisture filled her eyes.

"Sharon, I do love you," he said and moved his hands to her face where his thumbs gently wiped away the wetness spilling down her cheeks. "I need you," he whispered against her lips.

Sharon felt herself yielding to his kiss, to his closeness, but she knew she had to resist. Had she learned nothing through the years? For a moment, she felt as giddy as that nineteen-year-old girl. But at least now, she would not act on impulse. She had learned the hard way about runaway emotions. *I am older. I am wiser,* she kept repeating while reveling in this closeness to Marcus.

She forced herself to move away. "Under the circumstances, there's no way it would work, Marcus. Marriage takes more than just love."

"I'm well aware of that, Sharon. But you and I are compatible, don't you think?"

She nodded and smiled.

"And I know you can't live here. But Bobby will grow up, you know. In two more years, he'll start kindergarten. I could handle a long-distance relationship for that long. I've been a widow for eight years, I think I could handle a couple more, although it would be difficult, now that I know you."

"But that's just it, Marcus." Her eyes pleaded with him, and she hoped she would not say the wrong things. He was saying a permanent relationship was possible, but she knew it was impossible. "There are things you don't know about me, Marcus. Things in the past. . ." she began and returned to sit on the edge of the couch.

"I know what I need to know, Sharon. You're a lovely caring Christian woman. We all have our weaknesses, our failings, our pasts."

She looked up at him. "Its not that I've done something so horrible, Marcus. But it's something you would have to know if I were to consider anything beyond friendship."

"And we can't go back to just that," he said flatly.

Sharon shook her head, knowing he was right and feeling the loss already.

He sat beside her and took her hands in his. "Then, by all means, tell me about the past," he prompted.

Sharon looked at their hands, then lifted her eyes to his. "I'm not sure it's the right thing to do, Marcus. I will have to give it some thought."

fifteen

Saturday, the day of the cookout, was a lovely day. Trish told herself she shouldn't be nervous. Normally, she wouldn't be. After all, it was only an informal cookout. Her dad and Marcus were the grill chefs. Both had come to the house for several evenings and made sure the grills were in place and in working order. Beside the patio tables, they'd brought up the folding tables that Marcus had left with the house since he had no need or room for them in his house.

Trish's mom and Melba made sure Trish purchased everything she'd need from the supermarket. On Saturday, her mom brought extra help, and it looked like everything should go like clockwork. The cookout had been about the only subject Trish and Luke had discussed all week, and it had been a refreshing change that Julie hadn't been the center of their conversations.

Even the boys were helpful. Kathleen came around two o'clock. She and Bo would take the boys to the zoo right after they finished eating, which pleased Caleb and Mark.

"Bobby's not in the hospital anymore. Mom took us to see him at his home. Can he go with us?" Mark asked.

"He's not strong enough yet," Marcus said. "Why don't you get out the croquet set? Some of the guests might like to play, and they'll start coming before long."

Marcus walked over to Trish, who was setting out plates on the long tables. "Sharon's cookies will make a good addition, Trish. You'll be pleased."

"Oh, I'm sure I will," she said. "How are things with you two?"

"Now that Bobby's been released from the hospital, Sharon's busier than ever, even though she does have Lisa helping."

"I mean personally, Marcus."

Marcus nodded. "I suppose you could say we're at a crossroads, Trish." He stood thoughtfully for a moment, then said nothing more. He shrugged.

Trish felt she knew what he meant. She and Luke seemed to be at a crossroads, and she wasn't always sure what step to take or what direction to turn. She gave her father-in-law an encouraging squeeze on the arm. "Well, I'd better get changed before the guests arrive," she said, turning back toward the house.

"Trish!" her mom exclaimed a few minutes later when Trish walked into the kitchen. "How chic. You could have stepped out of the pages of *Vogue*."

"Yes," Melba agreed. "You're so pretty."

"What? In this old rag?" she joked, uncomfortable with the compliments which made her realize she must run around looking like a hag most of the time. No wonder Luke's eyes wandered. *Watch it,* she warned herself. *There's no real evidence of that. He sees me quite well, as a matter of fact. He just doesn't like what he sees.*

Actually, the outfit was new. White linen pants paired with a short-sleeved sailor-cut top with a wide collar. A thin strip of red binding bordered the collar and the gold buttons down the front. Chunky white sandals were the perfect accessory. Her figure was still great, thanks to swimming and running after the boys.

Her honey-blond hair fell in soft natural waves to below her shoulders and tucked behind her ear on one side. She'd enhanced her sea-green eyes with mascara, applied peach-colored lip gloss, and added small gold earrings. Of course she knew it was the inside that counted, but it was the outside that made first impressions. She admitted that her inner self hadn't been too attractive for awhile, and she hoped to impress Luke in some way.

"Who is this beautiful creature?" Marcus said when Trish stepped back out onto the patio. Trish felt a blush as Luke's head turned. He gazed at her curiously. Then he smiled.

"You look great, Trish. Really good."

"Thank you, gentlemen," she said brightly and turned toward the tables. Her heart sang. Luke hadn't complimented her in a long time. Maybe tonight they could recapture some of the romance that had gone out of their marriage.

Paul and Jan Thomas were the first guests to arrive. Soon after, others came, including Julie and a couple of other residents. Julie was very pretty with her shoulder-length medium brown hair framing a classic oval face. Her light brown eyes weren't outstanding. Neither was her conservative denim skirt or white short-sleeved cotton shirt. But everything about Julie was attractive, especially her bubbly personality.

Everyone seemed to like her. And of course, she and Luke engaged in conversation. It would have seemed strange if they hadn't. Trish refused to watch, as if she would catch a suspicious look or a gesture.

Before long, the house, patio, pool, and yard were filled with people having fun. While Luke made sure he went around and talked to everyone, Marcus and Trish's dad were busy at the grills. Soon, Sharon appeared with a huge tray of cookies. Trish smiled, seeing that the look passing between Marcus and Sharon was special. She saw how Sharon lowered her eyelids and a becoming blush colored her cheeks.

"Try a bite and see if you approve," Sharon prompted when Trish walked over.

Trish broke off a bite of a cookie. "These are not good, Sharon, they're superb. You made them?"

"My mom's secret recipe," Sharon said, happy to share something of her mother with someone else. "I've changed it a little to reduce the fat."

"Oh, well. I'll have more than a bite," Trish said, taking the rest of the cookie. She touched her stomach. "I forgot to eat lunch."

"From the looks of this spread," Sharon complimented, "I have a feeling we'll all stuff ourselves."

After everyone was settled in their choice of eating places, Trish tried to make sure everything was running smoothly. She was seated at an end spot next to Jan. Luke was farther down between a couple of colleagues. Julie and the two residents sat together at the other end of the table. Noticing that some iced tea and lemonade glasses needed refilling and everyone was engrossed in conversation, Trish got up for the pitchers.

She noticed that Julie's hand seemed to shake as she held up her glass for a refill. Trish poured, Julie put the glass to her lips, and Trish walked on by.

She stopped, hearing Julie say, "Oh, I'm so clumsy." A huge spot of tea was spreading over her white shirt.

"I had the glass too full," Trish said, trying to be the

perfect hostess. "I'm sorry."

"I would like to wash it off, if I might," Julie said.

"The bathroom is right inside the sliding glass doors, to the left of the game room," Trish said.

"Thanks, I'll find it."

The incident bothered Trish. A pediatric surgeon's assistant, who must have steady hands, spills her tea? Had shaky hands? It just didn't fit. *Something* had caused Julie to be unsteady! *Being at Luke's house? Or. . .being around Luke's wife?*

After returning the pitcher to the table, Trish went into the house and knocked on the bathroom door. "Did you find everything you need, Julie?"

"Oh, yes, yes, thanks. I'll be right out."

"No hurry," Trish replied.

Soon, the door opened, and the smiling assistant emerged, looking sweet and calm and guilty as sin. *Guilty,* Trish thought. *Of what? Of wanting my husband? I mustn't do that—get all worked up over nothing. She's just embarrassed over spilling her tea. Everyone does such things. Let's just hope a pediatric surgeon isn't that clumsy in the operating room.*

≈

Marcus wanted Sharon to feel welcome and at home during the cookout. He needn't have been concerned. As he took her around to introduce her, he discovered that all the guests had either met her or knew about her from the extensive news coverage about Bobby and the accident.

They all wanted to know how Bobby was adjusting, now that he'd gone home. Sharon graciously repeated the answer over and over, saying his adjustment was remarkably good. He'd already adjusted to his nurse, Lisa, in the hospital and was happy to have her helping care for him.

Marcus needn't have worried about Sharon's feeling comfortable. Almost before he knew it, she was walking around the pool with Trish's mom and Irene Thomas, conversing as if she'd known them for a long time. She apparently made friends easily. That didn't surprise him. He'd wanted to be her friend from the very beginning. Now he didn't want it to stop there.

When Luke summoned the crowd to the food, Sharon walked toward Marcus. His heart skipped a beat as if he were a teenager again. She looked up at him with a sparkle in her blue eyes and warmth in her smile.

"Thank you for inviting me, Marcus," she said. "This is so nice. I think it's just what the doctor would have ordered."

"What the judge ordered," he returned, and they both laughed.

He gestured for her to go ahead of him for a plate. His thoughts, however, went beyond this evening. Now that he'd found her, he couldn't imagine being content without her. For an instant, another thought crossed his mind. What could possibly have been so awful in her past?

sixteen

As each day passed, Sharon could detect rapid improvement in Bobby. Soon, Luke would say he was able to travel. What should she do about Marcus? What could she do? Simply say she could not marry him, offering no explanation, and go to California? If they married, they could have a good life together, but not unless they faced the truth of their pasts. The truth might drive him away, but she could not keep something like this from him.

What to do? *Dear Lord*, she prayed, *guide me*.

If she married Marcus, she would still have to be near Bobby until he was old enough to accept Mary and James as his caregivers, assuming they got custody. Would Marcus move to California? Or would they have a long-distance marriage with infrequent visits until Bobby started school?

Sharon sighed. It all seemed too complicated.

Marcus had called a couple of times since the cookout, but he hadn't come over. Near the end of the week, he telephoned. "Sharon, I need to see you."

"Marcus, I haven't decided—"

"I'm not pressuring you, Sharon. I'd like for us to go for a short drive and a walk on the beach. There's something I have to tell you before this can go any further."

Sharon stared at the phone after hanging up. He sounded distressed. Perhaps he'd decided it was all too complicated. Suddenly her heart began to pound. Suppose, after she'd mentioned her past, he had delved into it. A judge would probably know how to do those things. Had he discovered this secret she had kept from him?

It was late afternoon, and Marcus was on his way. Bobby and Lisa were playing in the backyard. Lisa said she could stay as long as needed. Sharon didn't bother to change from her jeans, T-shirt, and sandals. She sat in the porch swing, waiting, as she had several months ago. Was this going to be another disaster?

Sharon didn't wait for Marcus to come to the porch, meeting him in the driveway instead. She got in the car. He smiled and greeted her, but the smile didn't reach his eyes. She had not seen him so concerned before. Marcus was one of those happy people with a ready smile. Not today.

His appearance was casual—he wore walking shorts, knit shirt, and sandals. But his manner was far from casual. He did ask about Bobby, and she gave a progress report. He nodded, but she felt his mind was miles away. Sure enough, he turned toward the beach a few blocks away, then took a side road that wound around in the direction of the fateful cottage.

Marcus parked at the side of the beach cottage that had the windows and doors boarded up. Pieces of roof were missing, and the banister had broken away from the corner of the house.

"This was my parents' cottage years ago," he said. "I haven't kept it up. It holds unpleasant memories for me."

Sharon knew he must be speaking of that night, twenty-three years ago. She looked away from the cottage and from him. He led her down to the outcropping of rock, where they could both could lean against the rocks and stare out over the foam-tipped waves of the ocean, licking at the sandy beach, then retreating.

"You spoke of the past, Sharon," he began distantly. "There is nothing in your past that could be worse than what I did."

Sharon's head turned to stare at him, opening her mouth to say that if he were speaking of twenty-three years ago, then it was a mistake they both shared—not just him. But Marcus stilled any words she might say with an uplifted hand and a sorrowful countenance.

He told her then, about the night a troubled young girl appeared on the beach, and he invited her into the cottage. How it had started innocently, had progressed to sharing of their problems, and resulted in intimacy. "I have never felt comfortable at the beach cottage since then."

Sharon felt it was because he regretted that night with her, but his next words left her cold. "When I awoke early in the morning, she was gone. Although I asked around, no one knew an Angela. I never found a trace of her." He took a deep breath, cleared his throat, and said in a strained voice, "I fear she walked into the ocean that night and never returned."

After a long moment he said, "I had the opportunity to help that girl, but I took advantage of her instead. I know the Lord has forgiven me, but I've never been able to completely forgive myself."

He turned toward her, and she saw his pain. "I've never told anyone about this. It would have hurt more than helped. But I wanted you to know that nothing in your past could be worse than this."

"Oh, Marcus," she said, feeling so touched that he confided in her. She knew instantly how cruel it would be not to tell him the truth. He should not be burdened with believing a young girl might have drowned because of him. She stood in front of him. "I know about that night, Marcus. Angela did not drown. That was not her real name. You see, I. . .am Angela."

He was shaking his head. "What are you talking about?"

"That night, I wanted to be anyone but myself, and chose the name Angela. I didn't want you to know I was only nineteen."

Sharon's eyes misted over. "You see, Marcus. We share the same guilt."

He stared at her, dumbfounded. "You're not surprised, Sharon. Then you have known, all along, who I was."

"Yes. It wasn't difficult finding out that the Sinclairs owned the cottage. The phone book listed a Marcus Sinclair. A few weeks after that night, I drove by the address given in the phone book. I saw you in the front yard with a pregnant woman and two small children."

"I'm so sorry you had to go through that, Sharon. I can say good came from it. That night changed my life. It caused me to make responsible decisions concerning my wife, my children, and my relationship with God. It seems your life has gone well too."

"It was hard at first. You see, I married Mitchell when Robert was five years old. I couldn't have asked for a better father or husband than Mitchell. The Lord has blessed me too, after I realized I needed Him so desperately in my life."

"So, Mitchell was your second husband?"

"No. I never married Robert's father."

"What happened? Did he not want to be a part of his son's life?"

Sharon swallowed hard. She began to shake her head. Her eyes clouded, and she bit on her lip. She would have fallen had Marcus not grasped her shoulders. She barely managed to utter the words: "I never wanted you to know."

"Know what?" he demanded. His hands dug into her shoulders.

"Marcus," she said pleadingly. "I got pregnant that night."

"What?" he rasped. He could only stare at her.

"I never intended to say anything, Marcus. I never expected to see you again or be involved with your family. I decided that years ago. But the accident changed all that. I haven't known what to do. I wanted Bobby to know you and your family. But I—"

He seemed to have turned to stone. Even his eyes didn't blink. He looked as if he were living a nightmare.

Sharon wrenched away from his hands. "I'll walk home. It's not far." She hurried around the rocks. She could feel his eyes following her, uncomprehending, unblinking. She began to run along the sand like she had so many years ago. She'd made another mistake, only this time she didn't have the excuse of innocence or youth.

Would that be her final memory of Marcus? How could she ever forget his eyes staring at her with a look of. . . what? Incredulity? Or loathing?

🙚

Marcus could not think clearly. A judge was supposed to be levelheaded, make difficult life-or-death decisions, but now his thoughts were a jumble, his emotions swirling like cardboard in a hurricane.

Marcus walked across the sand and down to the ocean's

edge, thinking about that night so long ago. He had stayed at the cottage for two more days, wondering if Angela would return, asking others in the area if they knew her. No one did. He'd looked out at the ocean, wondering if she'd walked into the ocean and perhaps never walked out again.

Guilt had assailed him. He'd been unfaithful to Bev, to his own sense of morality, to his claim of being a Christian. When it came to the testing time, he'd failed miserably. He had gotten on his knees and poured out his heart to God, asking forgiveness. Believing it best not to burden Bev with his guilt, he returned home and asked her to forgive him for putting his studies ahead of everything else. She promised to be more supportive of him. Both promised to try and be more understanding of the other.

For a long time fear remained in his heart. What happened to Angela? He'd searched the papers for an Angela, wondering if she'd washed up on the beach. At times, he hoped he had only imagined her.

Now, turning to stare at the rocks and the beach house, he knew he had not imagined that night, nor had he imagined what the consequences might have been for her. *A troubled girl came to me, and I took advantage of her,* he admitted to himself. *As a man, a married man and father, as a Christian, I should have given her hope, a place to turn. Instead, I thought of myself, pitied myself for having a wife who didn't understand my needs while she was saying I didn't understand hers. I drank, which lowered my inhibitions, and I was tempted. I yielded to a girl looking for answers, and instead I gave her more trouble.*

How much damage had he caused that young girl? No, he couldn't blame her for not telling him she was pregnant. Of course she wouldn't want him to know. What could she have expected of him? A married man who walked away from his wife and children when the going got tough. When Bev had ordered him out and said she was going to get a divorce, he should have told her no, that this was his home, she was his wife, those were his children. He had sworn before God to love and cherish, and that's what he should have done.

Instead, he'd taken a young girl's word that she was twenty-one. Would it have made any difference if he'd known she was only nineteen? Or would that only have enticed him further? He might make all kinds of excuses for his behavior. That happened in his courtroom every day.

Numb from the revelations, Marcus made his way up to the cottage. He pulled the boards from the front door quite easily. No doubt someone else had done so and made use of the cottage. He turned the knob and discovered he didn't need a key to get inside. Someone had broken the lock. The afternoon light shining through the doorway revealed the couch pushed closer to the fireplace than he had left it. Someone had left ashes in the fireplace. Otherwise everything seemed to be intact. It didn't matter.

He reached for the poker and stirred the lifeless ashes. Sharon was Angela? This woman he'd come to respect and even love had lied to him. Twenty-three years ago she had lied about her name, her age. And these past months, she'd kept the truth from him. *Why? Why?*

He shuddered, feeling a trembling through his body like chills of the flu. His hand shook so he missed the hook when trying to replace the poker. It clattered to the hearth like the realization clanging in his brain. Sinking into the chair, where he'd sat twenty-three years ago, with his elbows on his thighs, he covered his face with his hands.

Not only had Sharon lied to him, but she had denied him the knowledge of his own son for all these years. Her son, his son, had recently been killed, and he hadn't even known he had that son. It was not easy to absorb these facts.

Marcus stayed at the darkened cottage for hours, long after the light at the doorway turned to darkness. He grieved for the son he never knew, his own flesh and blood who was killed in that accident. He never got to see him, touch him, love him. *My son that I never knew is dead.*

And Sharon. She must have gone through much humiliation and suffering bearing a child out of wedlock, then rearing him for many years without a husband.

Another thought broke through. All the concern about Bobby's rare blood type. *Bobby,* he realized, *is my grandson.*

How could she help but harbor deep resentment toward him? And he could not blame her. Had she accepted his recent help because she felt he owed her and Bobby something? And of course. . .he did.

As the hours passed, Marcus could do nothing but face the truth, the facts. Then he wondered what he would do with the information. Was this some kind of second chance to make up for the hurt he had caused Sharon? Should he try and earn her forgiveness?

He thought of her rearing his child for five years without a father. Surely she must harbor some resentment toward him. That would explain her reluctance to respond to his admission of love. Now he could understand why she would not even consider a relationship with him. And who could blame her? Not Marcus!

Later at home, far into the night, completely awake after a restless sleep, Marcus stared through the darkness toward the ceiling. Like dawn breaking though the dark, he understood Sharon's reluctance to tell him about Bobby. Now he was faced with a dilemma. Was he going to share this knowledge or keep this secret from his own family?

seventeen

Deep inside, Marcus felt he knew what he should do, but dreading it, he procrastinated, telling himself he would wait until the Lord gave him a definite sign. No such sign came during the following days, and he threw himself into his work with renewed fervor.

On Sunday afternoon he lounged on the patio after lunch with Luke, Trish, and the boys. Each of them were subdued after they asked about Sharon and Bobby. Marcus said he hadn't seen them or talked with them for days, but he didn't elaborate.

Luke and Trish were quiet, lost in their own thoughts. Marcus watched the boys frolic in the pool, thinking about his grandchildren. What would it do to them, knowing he had another grandchild? He glanced over at Luke and noticed the strain on his son's face. How would it change Luke's estimation of him? And Trish? She respected him so much. Would that change?

Suddenly, Luke's beeper sounded. He reached for it. "Hospital," he said, picking up the cell phone and punching in the number.

"Julie?" he exclaimed, swinging his legs around and rising to a sitting position. Abruptly he stood and paced. "I'll be right there."

He faced Trish and Marcus with a look of disbelief on his face. "Julie's overdosed. I have to go." He left Trish and Marcus in stunned silence.

Julie's attending physician talked to Luke as soon as he could but didn't think it wise for her to have visitors just yet. "We pumped her stomach and are trying to get it all out of her system."

Luke could hardly believe it. Paul Thomas was on duty, and the older doctor pulled him aside, discussing what had happened as best they could piece it together.

Julie hadn't come down to begin her shift at 7:00 A.M. No one thought anything about it for awhile. She was on twenty-four-hour call and hadn't been able to go to her room until around 2:00 A.M.

Finally she was called on the phone, then beeped. There was no response. Paul Thomas had the pediatric head nurse go up to Julie's room. When there was no response, they had the cleaning lady unlock the door. Julie was still in bed, and the head nurse was unable to wake her. After seeing a pill on the floor beside the bed, her eyes lit upon two bottles on the bedside table. She picked them up. One was a no-doze prescription for Julie. The other was a sleeping prescription for Amy Smith, prescribed by Julie Dalton, M.D. The nurse knew immediately that Julie had either OD'd or a mixture of the pills had poisoned her system.

"Why would she do it, Paul?" Luke questioned, but they both knew. Going through med school was tough. Being a resident under constant scrutiny and on call for twenty-four- and thirty-six-hour shifts demanded all one could give. It wasn't easy, but those who couldn't handle it shouldn't be in medicine. It was a demanding profession that didn't end at five o'clock in the afternoon.

"Apparently she just couldn't handle it, physically or emotionally," Paul said.

"She had such great potential," Luke countered. "Why would she chance throwing it all away?"

"You know the answer, Luke. An intelligent woman like her wouldn't do this deliberately. Like others in the past, she thought she could handle it. But she got hooked."

Luke returned home after supper, and Trish warmed his meal up in the microwave. "Julie has a problem," he said, "but I don't know the details yet."

"I hope she'll be all right," Trish said.

Luke flashed a skeptical look in Trish's direction. He hadn't expected such a mild response from her. But she had simply turned and was pouring herself a cup of coffee.

"Marcus is calling a family conference," she said, sitting across from him.

"Those are rare. What's up?"

"He didn't say, but it sounds serious. When's a good time for you?"

Luke sighed. Tomorrow was going to be a trying day at the hospital. His brightest star had ceased to shine. "Now?"

"I'll see if Kathleen and Bo can come. Marcus didn't want the children around, so I'll send them next door if it's okay with Marge."

❧

Marcus knew Luke had a good heart and could never be totally objective about his patients, coworkers, family, or friends. He could understand having a colleague with whom you could relate about your profession in a way that you couldn't with those outside the profession. It formed a bond. That could easily have happened between Luke and Julie. And it would be easy for it to get out of perspective.

That was the deciding factor for Marcus as he had

debated what to tell his family about his earlier relationship with Sharon. Maybe if he could explain some of what had happened in his own marriage, it would help Luke with his. And too, the situation was not just a private matter between him and Sharon. He must do what he could for the woman who bore his child, who was caring for his and her grandson. He wanted no more secrets.

His family liked Sharon. Their acceptance and approval of her made Marcus feel it was safe to confess his one night of infidelity and his recently learning that Bobby was his grandson. Surely he could be forthright with his own grown children.

Kathleen and Bo had dropped everything to come right over. The boys were already at the neighbors by the time Marcus arrived. The six adults gathered at the round kitchen table, where important matters in the past had been discussed. Marcus accepted only a glass of water, and the others, sensing something serious, did the same.

Marcus took a sip of water. It went down the wrong way, and he had to cough and clear his throat.

Trying to make it easier, Luke asked, "Are you ill, Dad?"

Marcus gave a short ironic laugh. "Ill at ease, son."

Brian looked at his watch, and Marcus thought he'd better get on with it before Brian left for one of his numerous activities.

Marcus began. "This happened twenty-three years ago."

"Sure you don't want to talk to a priest instead of us?" Brian quipped with a grin.

"No, Son. It touches your lives too. It's not something I can keep to myself."

Hesitantly at first, and then with a stronger voice,

Marcus told about the early years of his marriage to Bev. Perhaps they'd married too young, right out of high school, but they'd felt their love would see them through anything. They hadn't planned to have children right away. Bev would work while Marcus went to law school.

"We never considered you a mistake, Luke," Marcus said. "But you didn't conform to our well-thought-out plans."

Luke nodded and smiled. He'd never doubted his parents' love and devotion for him.

"For several years, things were great. We even had another child." Marcus smiled at Kathleen, and his daughter returned the smile. "But later, when I was in law school, things got tough. Mom and Dad helped out with my schooling, and things were fine until about a year before I was to take the bar exam."

Marcus knew he could have blamed the problems on about anything that all married couples faced. After the wedding came a marriage. After the honeymoon came daily living. All those factors played a role. But he had to be honest.

"The biggest problem was that I put my career, my needs, my wants, ahead of all else. My reasoning was that I had to pass that bar exam for my family. That was true. But mainly it was for me."

He told about frequent arguments over nothing in particular. "Accusations were made. Bev was pregnant with Brian," he said. "That pregnancy was particularly difficult, and for months she suffered from morning sickness."

"So I was the mistake," Brian quipped, trying to lighten the mood.

Kathleen punched him on the arm. "Don't be silly,

Brian. You're no mistake." She made a playful face at him and kidded, "You just make everybody else sick."

Everybody laughed nervously. Apparently, the worst was yet to come. Marcus took another sip of water.

He set the glass down and continued. "Finally, Bev threw me out. She literally tossed some of my clothes out the door. Said she was going to file for divorce the next morning and she did not want me to show up on her doorstep or she'd shoot me. She made a believer out of me," Marcus said.

"At the time, I was happy to go. My whole life seemed like a mistake, and the only thing that could fix it was passing that bar exam." He shook his head. "What I did then is inexcusable."

Marcus stared at his folded hands on the table, rather than look into the eyes of his family. He didn't want to see any disgust, disappointment, disapproval from these people he so dearly loved.

He told them then about the night at the beach house, as stormy as his emotions. About Angela. About fearing she had drowned and blaming himself for his irresponsibility. About turning his life over to the Lord and starting over. Not even Brian attempted to crack a joke.

Marcus was quiet for so long, Trish said softly, "Dad." She only called him that when she was particularly fond of him. He smiled faintly.

"Everybody makes mistakes," she said.

He took a deep breath. "That's not all."

After another pause, he said, "Only a few days ago I found out that. . .Sharon is Angela. She was that girl." He told of how she had reared her child alone for five years and had never wanted him to find out because of how it could affect him and his family. He looked around at them all now. "Do you understand what this means?"

He saw instant comprehension in Luke's eyes. "Bobby's rare blood type," he said.

Kathleen gasped.

Marcus nodded. "Sharon's son, who was killed." His voice broke. Tears stung his eyes. "He was my son that I never knew. Bobby is my grandson. I'm sorry. I didn't think I'd get emotional." He took a handkerchief from his back pocket, wiped his eyes, and blew his nose.

"Are you and Sharon getting serious, Dad?" Brian asked.

"I thought we were, Brian. Now I think she wanted Bobby to be acquainted with me, with us. I couldn't blame her if she wants nothing to do with me personally."

"I have confidence in you, Dad," Brian said, using the words Marcus had said to him many times. "You'll work things out the right way."

Marcus looked around. Tears were streaming down Kathleen's cheeks. She looked over at Bo. "I guess we should go." She came over and hugged Marcus, but not with that special little squeeze she usually had for him.

Luke said nothing, nor did he look at Marcus. He simply got up from his chair and walked out of the room without a word.

Marcus strongly suspected he had accomplished nothing except to disillusion his daughter and alienate his older son.

eighteen

Several days later, Marcus called Sharon and asked if he could stop by after leaving the courthouse. She didn't ask if he would stay for dinner, instead telling him that Lisa could keep Bobby occupied while she and Marcus talked.

When he arrived, Sharon offered him a cup of coffee. They sat at the kitchen table where they could see Bobby and Lisa playing with a plastic horseshoe set.

"Sharon," he began, believing she must have resentment in her heart for him. "I can't say that I'm altogether sorry for that night years ago. It brought me into a renewed relationship with God and my family. It forced me to grow up and take responsibility like a man. It taught me about God's forgiveness and grace. I hope you can forgive me."

Sharon looked stunned. "I was just as much at fault as you, Marcus," she said, but he shook his head.

"You were a teenager. I was a twenty-eight-year-old married man."

"I knew right from wrong," she insisted. "I wanted revenge on my boyfriend and my dad. It was as if I were a different person that night. I didn't want to be myself, with my problems."

"Was your family supportive during those years when you were unmarried?"

"Very," she said. "In a way it brought them closer to each other and to me. The damage had already been done

141

to their marriage, but we all sat down and discussed the situation like reasonable adults. For a long time, all I had heard from them was bitter arguments. That changed. They assumed my boyfriend, Jimmy, was the father. I never told them differently, only that marriage to Jimmy was out of the question."

"I remember," he said, "how hurt you were about your father and the impending divorce."

"I suppose I never really got over my parents' separation. But I learned a lot, Marcus. My parents could make mistakes too and sin. I went to California and lived with my dad. He found a duplex apartment house so that I could live in one side with the baby. After his divorce was final, he and Barbara lived in the other side. Later, Barbara kept Robert while I worked.

"After I married Mitchell, my dad and Barbara moved to Hawaii. He died of a heart attack several years ago." She took a deep breath. "I thought it best to live in California. The last thing I wanted to do was cause any trouble for you or your family."

"They know now," Marcus replied, his brow furrowing.

"You told them?" When he nodded, she asked, "How did they take it?"

"Brian seems to separate himself from it, as if it's my business and not his. Kathleen is disappointed because I'm not perfect. Luke has become distant. He's cordial, polite, but it's like the closeness has gone from our relationship."

"I'm so sorry." Sharon laid her hand on his arm. "That is what I wanted to avoid all these years."

"But this is my doing, Sharon. Not yours. I have a responsibility to Bobby, and I will be as much of a grandfather to him as you will allow."

Two days later when Sharon and Lisa took Bobby for his checkup, Luke said the little boy had healed sufficiently to go California. Bobby should still be kept from any vigorous activity, Luke warned, but there was no reason he couldn't be allowed to run and play like any other healthy little boy.

Luke tried to be kind, considerate, efficient, and professional as always, but he knew he was treating Sharon differently. His suspicion that she had noticed the change was confirmed when she asked, "Could I speak with you privately, Luke?"

"Certainly," he said, after a long pause.

Lisa said she would take Bobby to see the nurses and some of the little patients he had met while hospitalized.

Sharon and Luke went into his office. He motioned for Sharon to take a seat, but she remained standing, saying this wouldn't take long. "Bobby and I will be leaving for California as soon as I can take care of a few things and book a flight."

"I see," Luke said, walking around his desk. His fingers touched the edge of the desk, and he looked up at her coldly.

"Again, I want to thank you for what you've done for Bobby," Sharon said. "And for your kindness. I also want you to know I've always wanted to avoid causing any problem for Marcus and his family."

Luke looked down, deeply distressed.

"I'm sorry," Sharon said softly.

"I'm sorry, too," he managed to say as she left the room. "I wish you and Bobby well."

Luke walked over to the window and stared out beyond

the rooftops of hospital wings. He hadn't been very cordial to Sharon, but he was trying to cope with the implications of his father's confession—trying to absorb the fact that he'd had a half brother he never knew, that Bobby was a blood relative. Caleb, Mark, and Bobby were all Marcus's grandsons.

Luke saw traffic far below, going forward while his thoughts traveled back in time. He'd had a good childhood, with memories of fun activities and loving parents. Now for the first time he allowed himself to think about that troubled time in his parents' lives. He'd heard some arguments but accepted that as a normal part of life. He sometimes got angry with his little sister who swiped his toys and tore his books.

But one night he'd awoken from a deep sleep and the sound was different. He heard his parents yelling at each other. He thought they hated each other, and he was scared. He'd heard his mom tell his dad to go away and never come back. Luke jumped out of bed to tell his dad not to go away, but when he got to the living room, he saw his mom throwing clothes out the door. His dad was driving away.

Afterward his mom fell against the slammed door and sobbed. Luke had gone over and tugged at her clothes until she noticed him. She turned and fell on her knees and put her arms around him. He tried to comfort her while she cried. He didn't know how, so he cried too.

When she put him back to bed, she told him it was just a bad argument and everything would be all right. He didn't think she believed that. He closed his eyes and she left the room, but he couldn't sleep. Later on, he kept remembering his dad's clothes lying outside in the rain. For a long time in his mind he saw the red taillights of the car that finally disappeared into the darkness.

Luke had thought his dad didn't love them anymore, and the days that followed were the worst days in his life. When he asked where his dad was, his mom said she didn't know. Then Dad came back. Things were different for awhile, like everybody was scared to talk too much and nobody argued. Then things got better than they had been before. There were more hugs and more fun, and Dad was home a lot more.

After that, Luke had never doubted his parents' love for each other or for him. His had been a good life. Now he realized he had blocked out that unpleasant time, never to deal with it. He must deal with it now.

Another factor he must deal with was that Sharon, the woman he had come to respect and admire, was the one with whom his father cheated on his mother. How would he deal with that?

"Luke?" came a voice behind him. He turned. There stood Paul Thomas.

"Is everything all right? You door was open and—"

"Sure, come on in, Paul. I was just. . .thinking."

"Yeah, this problem with Julie has us all concerned. I just heard her license has been revoked for writing the illegal prescriptions. And she's to be in treatment for a year."

That was something else Luke had to deal with. He was torn with disappointment in her and in himself. Accompanying that was a strong desire to help Julie, a bright, lovely woman who had taken herself along the road to self-destruction.

Is anyone who they appear to be? Sharon? My dad?

Julie? And, he added reluctantly. . .*even myself?*

ᴥ

Sharon knew this was not the time to make any decisions about her mother's house and car. Lisa was glad to accept the responsibility of the house and see that the grass was cut, hoping that Sharon and Bobby would return.

At almost the last moment, Sharon realized she hadn't returned Marcus's video camera. She called Trish, asking if she could drop it by since she would be leaving later in the day and wouldn't see Marcus.

Trish asked her to come early enough for them to talk and bring Bobby. She said the boys had been asking about him. Lisa offered to drive them since Sharon had already notified the police that she was leaving and the car would be parked beside the house.

Caleb and Mark were overjoyed to see Bobby. Lisa took the three boys out back to the patio. Sharon and Trish sat in the rec room, watching the boys play. Bobby had adjusted to his situation. How satisfying it was to see him play with his little relatives—something Robert had never had the opportunity to do. Sharon tried not to think how satisfying it would be if these grandsons of Marcus could grow up together. Pushing aside the thought, she handed Trish a sheet of paper.

"This is Lisa's address and phone number," she said. "Lisa has a key to the house. Anytime you want the bed and high chair, just let her know."

"Oh, Sharon," Trish said, moving to the edge of her chair, opposite where Sharon sat on the couch. "You will come back, won't you?"

Sharon shook her head. "I think I've done irreparable damage, Trish. I told myself I was doing what was best for Bobby. But it seems I've only brought difficulties to Marcus's family. I'm so sorry."

"Sharon, none of us hold against you and Marcus something that happened so many years ago. We were shocked. But that's because Kathleen and I both thought Marcus was perfect. I still respect him more than anyone I know. And so does Kathleen. She and Bo were over here the other night and agreed that Marcus has not been so alive in years as he is around you. We all like you, Sharon. Believe it or not, some of us haven't always been perfect."

They laughed lightly. "But that's not the point, Trish," Sharon argued. "It's not just a matter of a mistake years ago. The matter has been brought into the present. And from what I hear, Luke isn't accepting this very well."

Trish sighed. "Things at the hospital are occupying his mind right now, Sharon." Trish felt she would like to confide in Sharon, but reconsidered. Luke hadn't yet given Trish all the details about Julie. He'd told her not to talk about it. A hospital's reputation was at stake.

"He seemed distressed, and Marcus said he was distant toward him."

"Don't blame yourself, Sharon. Marcus is not upset with you. He's upset with himself and sorry he didn't know about your son. He's an honorable man and doesn't take his responsibilities lightly."

"I know," Sharon said, standing. "But I'm afraid I've hurt him personally. It was wrong of me to let things go so far."

A short while later, Lisa drove Sharon and Bobby to the airport. Sharon kept wondering if Trish might have called Marcus and perhaps he would show up at the airport to see them off.

One last glance before boarding the plane indicated that hadn't happened. She busied herself with explaining everything to inquisitive, excited Bobby, who kept calling the plane a big bird that ate people. Sharon laughed with him, enjoying the game and his wonderful healthy imagination.

Behind her laughter, however, was a nagging feeling. While they rose high in the air over Charleston, already Sharon missed the gentle people and soft southern skies of the area that deep in her heart was home.

&

Marcus had been in court all day. This was a difficult case, and he had to struggle to keep his mind off personal matters. He'd had files to read, matters to consider, and he'd hoped he could get a few hours sleep before beginning another day of trial.

When Trish called, he was surprised. His family didn't bother him during a trial unless it was an emergency. "What's wrong, Trish?"

"I just wanted to let you know Sharon dropped your video camera off at my house."

He felt like a dark cloud hovered over him. "I guess that means she doesn't want me going to her house."

"Marcus, she's gone."

"Gone?"

"Yes. She and Bobby left this afternoon for California."

Her words hit him like a bolt of lightning. Gone. Sharon and Bobby were gone. He had to do something, say something. For the life of him he couldn't remember her ever saying what part of California she lived in. "Trish, did she give you her address or telephone number?"

"No. And I didn't think to ask. I assumed you would know. Maybe Luke has it."

Marcus called.

"There was no reason for me to ask for it, Dad," Luke said.

"Do you remember the names of Bobby's maternal grandparents? Mary and James something."

Luke thought. "I was introduced to them, but sorry, I don't remember. If I think of it, I'll let you know. But she'll be in touch with you, won't she, Dad?"

"I don't think so, Son. She wouldn't impose herself on people who don't seem to want her around."

"Dad," Luke said after a moment, "I'm about ready to leave here. Would you stop by the house before you go home?"

"Sure," Marcus said blandly. He felt as if all the life had gone out of him. He'd pick up his video camera and go home. Sharon would have taken the tape. Someday she might show it to Bobby and tell him that man was his grandfather. A man who was very busy—judging others.

A short while later, Marcus pulled in the driveway right behind Luke. At Luke's bidding they walked around the house and out onto the patio, near the pool.

"I want to apologize, Dad," Luke said. "Looking back, I realize I've probably given the wrong impression to both you and Sharon. Frankly I expected you two to continue your relationship whether or not I approved." He walked over to a chair and sat down. "Some things aren't easy to admit, especially to one's dad."

Marcus sat opposite him. "It's just as difficult for a dad to confess to his son. But family members are the ones we should confide in."

Luke nodded, took a deep breath, and plunged in. "My attitude toward you and Sharon wasn't because of you at all, but because I could see so much of myself in your story about the past. I remembered seeing Mom unhappy during those days. I remember the arguments and how they made me feel."

"I'm so sorry," Marcus said.

"I know. I'm not saying this as a condemnation. I'm trying to confess."

They smiled at each other. "Sorry," Marcus said again.

"I, uh, got things out of perspective for awhile. My work, my time, my life became top priority. I haven't given the kind of thought to Trish and the boys like I should. So I want to thank you for telling us about your past. I'm going to get myself back on track." He stood, and Marcus joined him.

"Dad," Luke added, "I'm in total agreement that you have an obligation to Sharon and Bobby. In case it means anything, you have my blessing on whatever decision you make."

"It means everything, Son," Marcus said. "But I don't know how I can ever find a Sharon Martin who might be anywhere in the entire state of California."

⁊⦿

Trish saw Marcus and Luke embrace, and it thrilled her heart. The two men she loved most in the world should not be at odds. As soon as they came through the door, she gave Marcus a slip of paper.

"I remembered that Sharon gave me Lisa's phone number. She has Sharon's address and phone number."

Marcus looked at it like it was his long, lost friend.

"You staying for dinner?" she asked.

"Dinner?" He was studying the address and phone number. "No, I have a lot to do this evening at home. Big trial going on, you know."

"Well, you have three extra hours," Trish said, ignoring the remark about the trial. "We're on a different time zone than California."

nineteen

Mary and James met Sharon and Bobby at the airport and drove them home. Their teens, Steve and Kim, were waiting at Sharon's home with a big "Welcome Home" sign outside in the yard. Attached to the sign, huge helium balloons danced in the breeze, displaying bright colors of red and yellow, white and green, blue and orange.

After hugs and kisses and words of welcome, they went into the kitchen to be greeted by crepe paper streamers, a stack of presents, Barney tablecloth, plates, cups, and a birthday cake for Bobby. The teens had also stocked Sharon's cabinets and refrigerator with groceries.

Before long, Bobby was interacting with these relatives he hadn't seen in months as if there had been no separation. After the party, Kim bathed Bobby and got him ready for bed. With the time difference, it was past his bedtime. Steve offered to clean up the kitchen.

Sharon filled Mary and James in about Bobby's recovery and how well he had adjusted to his environment. The other couple didn't even offer for Bobby to spend the night with them. Sharon wondered if that was because they thought his time with her would soon end. Sharon knew they would try to make a smooth transition if they gained custody, and Sharon knew that would only prolong her distress.

These were good, loving people and the only thing hanging over this wonderful reunion was the impending custody case, which no one mentioned.

The matter of custody, however, was uppermost in Sharon's mind. Later that night, after Bobby was asleep and Sharon stood in the doorway of Robert and Karen's room, the ring of the telephone shattered the silence.

Sharon hadn't informed any of her friends about her return to California, so she wasn't expecting any calls. Perhaps Mary had forgotten to tell her something. Or worse, maybe she and James expected Bobby to be asleep by now, and they wanted to talk about the custody case after all.

Trembling, Sharon picked up the phone. A man's voice answered. "Marcus?" she questioned, when he said her name. His voice sounded strained as he apologized for not contacting her before she and Bobby left. He would be tied up with a court case for at least a week longer.

"I'm so grateful to you, Marcus," Sharon said, trying to put him at ease, "for being there when I so desperately needed someone."

"Sharon, I will come to California for the custody hearing, testify on your behalf, and relate my own personal desires and obligations to be involved in Bobby's life."

Sharon was touched by that and hardly knew how to respond. Her heart ached to think that his affection for her had waned. Yet she had to keep Bobby uppermost in her mind.

"Thank you, Marcus. I will consult with my attorney and see what he thinks best. How is your family?"

"I truly believe our relationships are growing stronger, Sharon. It seems they had set me up as some superdad. They're beginning to see me as a human being who needs them as much as they need me."

"And Luke?"

"It seems Luke wasn't upset with our situation at all. His concerns were both personal and work-related."

&

Sharon was glad to hear that the deep love and respect Marcus and Luke had for each other had prevailed. That was doubly confirmed a few days later when she got a letter from Luke.

"I regret," he wrote, "due to my own personal preoccupation that I did not communicate better with you and that my attitude was misconstrued as belligerence toward you and Dad. If you can accept us, with all our faults and failings, my siblings and I would feel honored if you will allow us, Bobby's relatives, to be involved with the two of you."

Sharon cried at this wonderful show of acceptance. Bobby should be allowed to grow up knowing his relatives. But how difficult it would be to see Marcus, now that she had foolishly allowed herself to fall in love with him. However, she must push her own feelings aside and do what was best for her grandson. Too many people would suffer if she didn't allow Marcus and his family to be involved with Bobby.

A couple of days later, after dinner with Mary and James, the teens took Bobby outside so the adults could talk privately.

Sharon knew this was the time. She had prayed about it. She knew facts would come out in court, that her past would be revealed, and that such information could well damage Mary and James's opinion of her. She wanted them to hear it firsthand.

She told them about that night twenty-three years ago,

about Mitchell not being Robert's birth father, and about how she had married him when Robert was five years old.

Mary and James sat as if enthralled or perhaps stunned like watching some kind of soap opera unfold before their eyes. Sharon told them that Marcus had asked her to marry him, but she couldn't do that just to improve her chances of getting custody of Bobby. She ended by saying that Marcus had called and was willing to come to California to help her.

"Regardless of what happens with the custody," Sharon said. "Bobby should be allowed to know his daddy's relatives. But I want you to know I intend to stay in California. I know Bobby needs us all."

"Was it serious between you and the judge?" James asked.

"It might have been," she admitted. "But I couldn't expect him to give up his job and come here, away from his grandchildren, in order to be with me and mine. And I can't leave Bobby."

"Oh, Sharon," Mary said, "you always put everyone else first and yourself last." Whatever else they might have said was halted when the children came in from outside.

❦

The following day, Mary and James stopped in. Kim was with them and took Bobby out for ice cream.

"We've given this a lot of thought, Sharon," James began.

"And what you told us yesterday has brought us to a definite decision," Mary added.

Great dread washed over Sharon. Her confession had probably damaged her character in their eyes. Perhaps they had even talked with their attorney, and he had told them their chances were better than ever.

"We talked of getting custody of Bobby primarily because we wanted you to feel free to make a life for yourself, Sharon," Mary said. "You selflessly devoted your life to Robert and Karen. They lived with you. You became their housekeeper, cook, and baby-sitter. You were more like a mother to our daughter than we were."

Mary wiped her eyes, and James took up the conversation. "The thought of custody came to us that first night we saw you with the judge."

Mary sniffed. "You two seemed to belong together. We wanted to give you every chance of making a life with someone. We doubted that a middle-aged man would want to take on a little boy."

"But you said the judge is going to take on the responsibility, regardless?" James asked.

Sharon nodded, looking from one to the other. Was she dreaming?

"We want you to know that we weren't trying to hurt you, Sharon. We were trying to help you," Mary said.

James added quickly, "We are willing to take care of Bobby. But honestly, we would never put you through something like a court case."

"It's not easy for me to be as loving and giving as you, Sharon," Mary confessed. "But James and I want to try. We love Bobby, and his being Karen's child and part of us is something we can't ignore. But he is yours in every sense of the word."

Sharon looked from one to the other as they took turns talking. It was James's turn.

"We haven't bonded with Bobby the way you have,

Sharon," he said. "And if you can find happiness in the South, if you want to take Bobby back there, then you have our blessing. I think he has forgotten much of his life here already. Go back if you want. We can visit back and forth. Just know we're behind you, whatever you decide to do."

A flood of tears washed Sharon's cheeks. She'd always known Mary and James were wonderful people. Now she knew they also had hearts of gold.

Two weeks later, Sharon did what she felt was right. She put her house up for sale and called Lisa.

"Can you meet us at the airport? Bobby and I are coming home."

twenty

Luke had done a lot of soul-searching over the past few weeks. It was time he acted on what he knew was right. He hadn't seen Julie since the day she lay in the hospital bed, looking so pale and lifeless. She had refused to meet his eyes or offer an explanation. She was in rehab now.

He had often compared her to Trish. He had found it refreshing to see lovely Julie, neat, never disheveled. She never complained, was always efficient, bright, happy. But he hadn't gotten past the surface appearance. He'd missed the signs that one of his own residents was under too much stress, choosing instead to indulge in a fantasy.

He and Trish were having a lot of discussions these days. They were praying about their marriage instead of arguing. One early morning, before the boys were up, they slipped out on the patio with coffee.

"I've been thinking about Julie a lot," Luke said. "Maybe God put her in my path so I could help her. As a doctor, and having been an intern myself, I should have recognized some of the signs of her problem. No one can go through those long hours without sleep and always be efficient, bright, cheerful." He shook his head at his own lack of insight. "In spite of the drugs, she has great potential, Trish. I would like to help her."

"Have you been to see her in rehab?" Trish asked.

"No."

"Then do, Luke. Let her explain to you how she got into

that mess. You need to get all this settled in your mind. And if you don't mind, I'd like to visit her. Maybe I can help somehow. At least I can pray with her. When she's clean, maybe a letter of recommendation from you will help reinstate her license."

Luke blinked his eyes against the emotion. His wife was a wonderful woman. "Have I told you lately," he said in a low voice, "that I love you?"

Trish rose from her chair and went over and bent down until her face was close to his. "And I love you," she said, her voice as soft as her lips became against his. After a long moment, she moved away. "Would you like to go for a swim?"

"I'd rather watch you," he said.

Trish threw off her robe, revealing a swimsuit underneath. She ran to the edge of the pool and dove in.

Luke watched his beautiful, graceful wife swim several laps before climbing out of the pool, laughing as she leaned to the side and wrung the water from her hair. The water drops on her tanned skin gleamed in the early morning sunshine. "Gives me energy for the day," she said.

Luke stared at her, as if he hadn't seen her in a very long time. Perhaps he hadn't. But standing there, she was full of life, exuberant, ready to face the day and two active boys. She was tired at night, just as he was, just as most human beings were, but she was honest about her feelings and her limitations.

How could he have been so blind? He stood as she walked closer. "I love you, Trish."

Her eyes studied his for a moment. Then he saw that mischievous gleam in hers that hadn't been there in a long time. "Of course," she teased, "why wouldn't you?"

His arms came around her. "You'll get wet," she warned.

"Who cares?" he said, pulling her closer.

"Mom, what's for breakfast?" they heard from the doorway.

Trish laughed. "They care."

"They, my dear, can wait. Their parents are busy at the moment."

Their lips met in another lingering kiss, making up for a long dry spell.

೩

Sharon had called to let Marcus know she had returned. He said he would stop by as soon as the trial ended. Another week passed, before there was a guilty verdict. Marcus came after supper and played with Bobby in the backyard, while Sharon made a batch of the cookies that the two guys liked so much.

After cookies and milk, Marcus helped with Bobby's bath and read him a bedtime story. "He's sound asleep," Marcus said, coming into the kitchen.

"Trish took me to the Christian preschool today. She's considering enrolling Mark for this fall. Do you think I should consider that for Bobby?"

Marcus pulled out a chair and reached for a cookie. "It was good for Caleb. The teachers are all Christians and they teach in fun ways. Every minute is scheduled, and children learn how to share and how to relate to each other."

"Yes, I saw the schedule, and it looks wonderful. I just wonder if Bobby is too young."

"It's only three hours in the mornings," Marcus said. "Why not enroll him, and if you aren't pleased, you can keep him at home."

"Now that's sensible," Sharon said and laughed.

"I'm glad you came back to Mount Pleasant, Sharon," Marcus said.

She nodded. "So am I. Bobby's happy here. And I'm glad he can know you and your family. You're a wonderful grandfather."

"It's not difficult, with a lad like Bobby. It's obvious he's had a good upbringing. Could I take some of these?"

"That's why I baked them," she said.

"In that case. . ." He picked up the platter stacked with cookies.

Sharon playfully hit his arm. "Put those down. I'll get a bag for them."

Marcus laughed. "Reminds me of wallpapering days."

Sharon quickly turned, afraid she might let her feelings show. For an instant she had felt so comfortable with Marcus that she almost forgot there would be no connection between them except as the grandparents of Bobby. After Sharon put cookies in a sandwich bag, Marcus took them, thanked her, and said good night.

Sharon felt lonely after he left. There had been no talk of love or marriage since her confession to him about the past. But she mustn't have regrets. Instead, she must count her numerous blessings.

Sharon couldn't have expected the additional blessing that occurred the following day. Marcus called during the morning. "Luke wants the two of us to meet him in his office around noon," he said.

Fear struck her heart. "Is something wrong? Has something come up about Bobby?" Why else would Luke want to see them together?

"No, nothing like that. You know Bobby's last examination showed a healthy little boy who has recovered completely." Marcus paused for a deep breath. "The boy who received Robert's corneas wants to meet you."

"Oh," Sharon said. "I didn't expect—"

"I know. I'll pick you up."

"Yes, I don't think I could drive. I'll call Lisa to stay with Bobby."

❧

Sharon didn't think she had ever been so nervous. Marcus held onto her arm as they walked down the hospital corridor and stopped at Luke's door. "Just a moment," she said and closed her eyes a moment for a prayer and a deep breath. "Okay."

Marcus opened the door and let her pass in front of him. Luke stood from where he sat behind his desk. Three people rose from the couch. A middle-aged couple and a young man. All three began to cry as Luke introduced them as the Edwards and their son, Tim.

"We promised each other we wouldn't cry," Mrs. Edwards said. "We couldn't come before now. We just weren't able to emotionally."

Mr. Edwards pulled a handkerchief from his pocket and blew his nose. "Nobody could have given our son a greater gift than. . ." He paused, cleared his throat, then spoke brokenly, "Than your son did, Mrs. Martin."

Sharon trembled with emotion, and Marcus put his arm around her shoulders and led her to one of the additional chairs Luke had brought in earlier. Marcus sat in a chair next to her. Luke handed her a tissue. Marcus reached for the box, and Sharon saw that tears had bathed his face.

They all sat except Tim. Sharon was afraid he might fall, for he looked as trembly as his voice. That didn't matter. His words of gratitude came from his heart. "I practiced what I would say," he began, "but I don't remember it now. I just know I was blind, and now I can see."

His breath came in short gasps. "That's from the Bible. And it's how I feel. I don't know why I got to live and your son. . ." He chewed on his lower lip and looked at the floor where his teardrops fell.

"I don't know either," Sharon said. "It wasn't God who caused the accident, any more than He caused your blindness. God could have prevented both, but He didn't. Sometimes we are the cause of our troubles; sometimes we are victims. But I know, for those who love God and have faith in Him, He works in all these circumstances. I'm glad you have Robert's eyes. Robert would be glad. Let me see. . .your eyes."

The young man slowly lifted his head and looked at Sharon. She smiled through her tears. "Robert would be pleased."

"I hope so. And I want you to be. And his little boy. If I can be a big brother to him, then I want to."

"I might take you up on that," Sharon said and saw a light appear in Tim's eyes—her son's eyes.

"I may seem young to you," Tim said, "but this changed my life. I was a Christian before the accident, but in a way it was like my life was dark too. I didn't live like a Christian. I thought life should be a party and someday I'd change."

He shook his head. "This changed me. The accident made things worse. I hated everybody, and God, and life. Now, I can see and. . .God has called me to tell other people about this. I hope your son would be pleased."

"Oh, he would," Sharon said. "I know he must be looking down and smiling on you right now. And I'm so pleased that a part of my son is still alive in you. Robert always wanted to make a difference in the world. Now he's doing that in such a unique way."

Tim finally sat down on the couch between his parents. "I won't have much free time, but if you would let me, I'd like to be kind of like a big brother to Bobby. Did he like the teddy bear?"

"Oh, yes, but I've told him it's from a very special friend, and he keeps it in a special place. Someday, I will explain the significance to him. Thank you for that."

"That bear has been his best friend since Tim was a wee lad," his dad said.

"Not anymore," Tim said. "Jesus said there's no greater friend than one who lays down his life for another." His voice broke, and his eyes misted over again.

"We know," Sharon said, nodding.

The group exchanged hugs, addresses, phone numbers, and expressions of gratitude for the meeting. Luke closed the door behind the Edwards family, then turned to Marcus and Sharon.

"As tragic as it is, Sharon—and I know your loss is great—I want to say that your son. . ." He looked at them both, "And my brother Robert has made a positive difference in the Edwards family, in those other donor recipients, in my family, and in myself. I am grateful for that. This is an example of God taking a tragedy and bringing good from it. I don't have a mother, and I wonder, could I have a motherly hug?"

Sharon fell into his outstretched arms, and it was as if she embraced her son. Particularly when Luke said, "I can't replace Robert, but I am here for you. Please know that."

Sharon moved away and looked into his eyes. Yes, Robert's brother was sincere. And he was right. So much good had come from that tragic mistake years ago and again from this recent tragedy. Physical life could be devastating. Spiritual life could be rejuvenating. She shared those thoughts with Marcus on the way home.

"I agree," he said. "And Luke expressed it well. Sharon, I'm proud of my son Robert. And I thank you and Mitchell for giving him a good life. I couldn't have done better."

"We shouldn't make comparisons, Marcus. Your children are fine."

"Yes, they are," he said and smiled. "But someday, I'd like for you to tell me all about Robert."

"I would love to do that. Most people are afraid to mention him, lest they make me sad. But I want to talk about him, remember him."

"Would you read that flyer to me again, Sharon? I want to be a donor too."

Sharon read and Marcus, thinking of Robert and Tim, found a couple sections of particularly significant.

> *Give my sight to the man who has never seen*
> *a sunrise, a baby's face or love in the eyes of a*
> *woman. Give. . .to the teenager who was pulled*
> *from the wreckage of his car, so that he might live*
> *to see his grandchildren play.*

 è

Later that week, Marcus went with Sharon to the courthouse, and they sat in a judge's private chambers. With the written consent of the maternal grandparents, Sharon was given permanent custody of Bobby. Marcus didn't mention legal visitation rights for himself, knowing he had no rights in this matter—only obligations.

The next Saturday, Luke and Trish took Bobby to the zoo with their boys and wanted him to stay overnight.

"That's asking a lot," Sharon said. "Three wild boys."

"I think I can handle it," Trish said, laughing.

"And I'm here to help," Luke reminded them. "Besides, there's a method to my madness. We will need you to reciprocate when I take Trish off on a second honeymoon cruise."

"Why haven't I heard anything about this?" Trish said.

"It was a surprise," Luke said. "What about the middle of next month?" His arm came around her and pulled her close to his side.

Trish looked up at him with loving eyes. "Anytime," she said, "would be perfect."

❧

Marcus awoke to a stormy Sunday morning. Lightning streaked the sky, and he heard a clap of thunder. It was a good day for covering up one's head, rolling over, and going back to sleep. However, it was the Lord's Day, and he should be in church.

After church, Trish invited Marcus over for lunch. "Sharon and Bobby will be there. He spent the night with the boys."

Marcus was eager to accept. During lunch the boys talked about the zoo. Bobby's eyes were big as he talked about a snake big enough to swallow him. But he liked all the animals, especially the big colorful tropical birds.

Marcus thought how much like a big, happy family they seemed to be. Grandparents, children, grandchildren. Only one thing would make it perfect. But would Sharon think so?

"You must rest, Bobby," Sharon told him when he protested about going home. He wasn't ready to leave his energetic, fun-loving cousins. Reluctantly, he said thank you and good-bye.

Marcus walked them to the car. The rain had stopped, but the sky was still overcast. After buckling Bobby in the car seat in back, he leaned down at Sharon's window before she started the engine. "Maybe the three of us could drive down to the beach after Bobby's rest period. There's something I'd like to show you."

"Yeah, yeah," Bobby whooped, and the two adults couldn't help but smile at each other.

"That sounded very much like an answer to your question, Marcus." She looked up. "But that sky looks ominous."

He was thinking her eyes were bluer than any sky, and he often wished he could read what lay behind them. They did tell him a lot. She was a warm, caring, wonderful woman who made him feel alive.

"The weatherman said it will clear."

"Oh, then, no problem," she teased, starting the engine.

Marcus moved back, laughing. "See you around five-thirty?" He knew she had supper around five.

"After such a great lunch, we'll have sandwiches. Want to join us?"

"Yes," he said, feeling as if the clouds had disappeared even though he could feel a few drops of rain splattering down. Holding out his hand, he saw the drops. Yes, there was such a thing as liquid sunshine.

twenty-one

Sharon was glad the sky was clearing. But she was uncertain about the direction Marcus was taking after their sandwich supper. She remembered how difficult things had become the other time they had gone to the cottage. She remained silent, however, as he continued driving toward the beach. Bobby was busy in the backseat with a bucket-shovel set Marcus had given him.

When the cottage came into view, Sharon could hardly believe it. It had a new roof, a new railing around the porch, and new steps. The broken windowpanes had been replaced, and it had a fresh coat of paint. "You've fixed it up!" she exclaimed.

Marcus pulled up beside the cottage. "I've had it renovated. And many of my evenings have been spent getting rid of the old furniture and cleaning up the inside. I had to do something with my lonely evenings while you two were away."

He was making it sound like he missed her as much as he missed Bobby. But she must be careful not to assume anything. "Maybe," he was saying, "you could give me some advice on furnishings."

Sharon didn't respond. She kept staring at the cottage. Just like so many lives lately, the cottage was being made new.

Marcus got out and took Bobby to a sandy spot in front of the cottage, and Bobby immediately began to dig. Sharon sat in the new swing on the porch. Marcus came up and sat beside her.

They both watched Bobby, seemingly trying to dig to China and finally reaching wet sand that he had flying all over himself. He was having such fun that they didn't have the heart to stop him.

Then Marcus began to speak of Cypress Gardens. "Several years ago it was destroyed by Hurricane Hugo. How devastating that seemed to be. But then something miraculous began to happen. New, exciting, unexpected growth began to appear. Sharon, although the gardens will be different than before, they will have just as great appeal."

His words seemed to have some kind of appeal in them. She turned and saw that his face had turned serious. "I wish, Sharon, that might happen with our relationship. I know you have experienced the effects of the past in a different way than I. But perhaps someday you can forgive me, even—" He stopped and looked up toward the scattered clouds.

"Love you, Marcus?" Sharon said in awe.

He looked at her again. "Yes. I don't want to ruin this wonderful relationship the three of us have. I don't want to pressure you. But Sharon, I love you."

"Marcus, I love you too. I love you for the fine man that you are. And I love you because. . .I just can't help it."

Joy spread over his face and disbelief filled his eyes. His hands grasped her arms. "Sharon," he said, "will you marry me?"

"Yes. Oh, yes." Her eyes filled with tears.

He took her in his arms and their lips sealed the promise of commitment. Their lips parted and Marcus held her head to his chest. They allowed themselves the flow of love that had no age or limits. Finally Marcus spoke again.

"I've never been to Scotland, my ancestral home. Does that sound like a good place for a honeymoon?"

Sharon straightened and held his hand. "I'd love to go to Scotland. But to begin our new life together, Marcus, I can't think of a better place than right here in this cottage. I can look back upon it as proof that God can turn a mistake into two of the finest blessings I've ever had—my son and my grandson." She paused. "Three blessings," she corrected. "I include you, Marcus. I do love you."

"I thought of that too, Sharon, but I was reluctant to suggest it." He drew her into his arms again, his chin touching the softness of her hair. A great burden had lifted from his shoulders—a burden of past irresponsibility. God has given him a second chance, and he felt the joy of loving Sharon and that precious child who was so intent on digging in the sand.

"Bobby," Marcus said suddenly, moving back. "I need to ask that young man's permission to marry you."

"Suppose he says no?"

"Where's your faith in me, woman?" Marcus jested and rushed down the steps like a young man.

Sharon watched as he knelt in front of Bobby. She couldn't hear what Marcus was saying, but she recognized the gesture when Bobby's mouth fell open in a huge "O" and his eyes widened. Then Marcus spread his arms, and Bobby fell into them, giving Marcus a big hug.

There was a glow about them. Sharon walked over to the railing and held onto it. Her eyes lifted toward the heavens. She caught her breath at the spectacular sight. Marcus and Bobby were silhouetted against an orange sun setting into the ocean. The clouds were gone. The storm was over. And shining down like a blessing from heaven was a golden sky.

A Letter To Our Readers

Dear Reader:

In order that we might better contribute to your reading enjoyment, we would appreciate your taking a few minutes to respond to the following questions. When completed, please return to the following:

Rebecca Germany, Managing Editor
Heartsong Presents
PO Box 719
Uhrichsville, Ohio 44683

1. Did you enjoy reading *After the Storm?*
   - ❑ Very much. I would like to see more books
     by this author!
   - ❑ Moderately
     I would have enjoyed it more if _____

   _____

2. Are you a member of **Heartsong Presents**? ❑Yes ❑No
   If no, where did you purchase this book?_____

   _____

3. What influenced your decision to purchase this
   book? (Check those that apply.)

❑ Cover	❑ Back cover copy
❑ Title	❑ Friends
❑ Publicity	❑ Other_____

4. How would you rate, on a scale from 1 (poor) to 5
   (superior), the cover design?_____

5. On a scale from 1 (poor) to 10 (superior), please rate the following elements.

    ___Heroine   ___Plot

    ___Hero   ___Inspirational theme

    ___Setting   ___Secondary characters

6. What settings would you like to see covered in **Heartsong Presents** books?_____

_____

_____

7. What are some inspirational themes you would like to see treated in future books?_____

_____

_____

8. Would you be interested in reading other **Heartsong Presents** titles? ❑ Yes   ❑ No

9. Please check your age range:
    ❑ Under 18   ❑ 18-24   ❑ 25-34
    ❑ 35-45   ❑ 46-55   ❑ Over 55

10. How many hours per week do you read? _____

Name _____

Occupation_____

Address_____

City_____ State_____ Zip_____

I Do

A Romantic Collection of Inspirational Novellas

Discover how two words, so softly spoken, create one glorious life with love's bonds unbroken. *I Do,* a collection of four all-new contemporary novellas from **Heartsong Presents** authors, will be available in May 1998. What better way to love than with this collection written especially for those who adore weddings. The book includes *Speak Now or Forever Hold Your Peace* by Veda Boyd Jones, *Once Upon a Dream* by Sally Laity, *Something Old, Something New* by Yvonne Lehman, and *Wrong Church, Wrong Wedding* by Loree Lough. These authors have practically become household names to romance readers, and this collection includes their photos and biographies. (352 pages, Paperbound, 5" x 8")

·········· Presents ··········

Hearts♥ng Presents
Love Stories Are Rated G!

That's for godly, gratifying, and of course, great! If you love a thrilling love story, but don't appreciate the sordidness of some popular paperback romances, **Heartsong Presents** is for you. In fact, **Heartsong Presents** is the *only inspirational romance book club*, the only one featuring love stories where Christian faith is the primary ingredient in a marriage relationship.

Sign up today to receive your first set of four, never before published Christian romances. Send no money now; you will receive a bill with the first shipment. You may cancel at any time without obligation, and if you aren't completely satisfied with any selection, you may return the books for an immediate refund!

Imagine. . .four new romances every four weeks—two historical, two contemporary—with men and women like you who long to meet the one God has chosen as the love of their lives. . .all for the low price of $9.97 postpaid.

To join, simply complete the coupon below and mail to the address provided. **Heartsong Presents** romances are rated G for another reason: They'll arrive *Godspeed!*